HARRY GERBER WAS SITTING ON MY STEERING WHEEL

He was two inches tall. A much smaller version of him was perched on the gearshift as well. And the tiny dots darting around on my dashboard—something told me they were a flock a tinier Harrys. All of them wore gray polyester suits, white shirts, and no neckties.

The little figure on the steering wheel hailed me with a cheerful wave of its tiny arm. "Hey, Fletch! Pretty slick, huh?" He sounded like Mickey Mouse. "I needed your encouragement, Fletcher. I've come back here to make sure you really are going to see me tomorrow. I remember that when you showed up tomorrow you'd seen me tiny in your car."

This was a strange mix of tenses. I thought for a moment. "You've invented time travel then?"

The little man on the dashboard glowed with pride. "Time travel's nothing. I'm the master of space and time, Fletch."

RUDY RUCKER

MASTER OF SPACE AND TIME

BAEN
SCIENCE FICTION
BOOKS

MASTER OF SPACE AND TIME

Copyright © 1984 by Rudy Rucker. Published in agreement with Bluejay Books from a Bluejay International Edition.

A Baen Book

Baen Enterprises
260 Fifth Avenue
New York, N.Y. 10001

First Baen printing, December 1985

ISBN: 0-671-55997-4

Cover art by James Warhola

Printed in the United States of America

Distributed by
SIMON & SCHUSTER
MASS MERCHANDISE SALES COMPANY
1230 Avenue of the Americas
New York, N.Y. 10020

For
Mike Gambone
and
Mary Molyneux

Contents

1

This Is the Name of This Chapter

My screen began flashing. I had the console rigged to measure quitting time to the nanosecond. Softech had a flexitime system, which meant that you could quit for the week after putting in forty hours. A few quick keypunches and I'd logged off for the weekend. I yawned and looked around the too-familiar room. I was pretty old to be working this hard. A couple of years ago I'd had it made—my own company and my own signature on the paychecks. But now . . .

"Finished so soon, Dr. Fletcher?"

It was my supervisor, an angular young blond woman named Susan Lacey. *Dr.* Lacey. No one used first names at Softech. Company policy.

"No, I'm not finished. But I've clocked in my forty hours. It's Friday afternoon."

She flashed her human-relations smile. "It's two

forty-seven, Dr. Fletcher. I don't have to tell you that they're in an awful rush for your program. You know how anxious they do get."

They. Lacey was always talking about her higher-ups as if it were her and me against some abstract impersonal *them.* It was her way of trying to win my sympathy, even though she was a slave driver. A pathetically transparent con job. I wished I could be my own boss again; I was too good for this noise.

"Don't worry." I snapped shut my briefcase. "The deadline's only Wednesday, you know. I'll bring the thing in under the wire. I always do."

All around me, my coworkers were still tapping away at their terminals. I was the only one with the nerve to take flexitime seriously. I'd never move up the Softech corporate ladder this way, but so what? All I needed from them was a steady paycheck. Soon I'd find a way to get my engineering firm back on its feet. I gave Lacey a curt nod and headed for the parking lot.

It was a hot day in late September. Buzzing around the trash cans were hornets, drunk with a summer's fatness. My car was the biggest on the lot—I had a black and white 1956 Buick, black on the bottom and white on top. Little Serena called it *Dada's saddle shoe.* I'd bought it just before Fletcher & Company went bankrupt, as a final present to myself. The guy I'd bought it from had gotten it off the original owner, a little old lady who only drove it to church, no lie.

As I unlocked my big old bomb, I noticed some things moving around in there. Bees? The biggest one was perched right on top of the white plastic steering wheel. But that was no bee. A wave of strangeness swept over me—a thick, airless feeling as if the world had suddenly turned into a giant movie set.

Harry Gerber was sitting on my steering wheel. He was two inches tall. A much smaller version of him was perched on the gearshift as well. And the tiny dots darting around on my dashboard—something told me they were a flock of yet tinier Harrys. All of them wore gray polyester suits, white shirts, and no neckties. Oh, my. Who else but Harry?

Harry Gerber: the out-of-it genius who'd been the inventor at Fletcher & Co. We'd had some wild times together, Harry and me. But now I hadn't seen him for over a year. He'd had a big fight with my wife Nancy—something about over-population and world hunger—and after that we'd drifted apart. He lived in New Brunswick, New Jersey, and I lived twenty miles away, in Princeton.

The little figure on the steering wheel hailed me with a cheerful wave of its tiny arm. "Hey, Fletch! Pretty slick, huh?" He sounded like Mickey Mouse.

I glanced over my shoulder to see if anyone from Softech was watching. Buzzing hornets and thick, sweet sun. I got in my car and closed the door. I took the thumb-sized Harry off my steering wheel and set him down on the dashboard. The smaller Harrys moved right along with him. They all stood there in a row, staring at me.

"Why all the copies, Harry?"

"I'm real, and the others are correction terms," said the thumb-sized man. "A convergent series of echoes. You've been reading *The Cat in the Hat Comes Back,* haven't you?"

"Yeah, I was reading it to Serena last night." I didn't bother asking how Harry knew. "You must be thinking about the scene where the Cat has a smaller cat in his Hat, and the smaller cat has a yet smaller cat in *his* hat, and the yet smaller cat has a still smaller cat, and so on forever, right?"

"You're a rational man, Fletcher. Watch this!" Each of the little Harrys squatted down by the next smaller one. The big one—the thumb-sized Harry—stuck some fingers in his mouth and attempted a sharp whistle. It came out as a wet hiss. But this was enough.

The smallest Harry I could see, a speck-sized one, jumped into the coat pocket of the next larger one, a flea-sized Harry. The flea-sized Harry jumped into the coat pocket of the ant-sized Harry. The ant-sized Harry jumped into the coat pocket of the thumb-sized Harry. They nested themselves together like Chinese boxes. I wondered how many levels there were.

"You like it better now?"

"I like it better."

"Aren't you going to ask me how I got this way?"

"I figure you'll tell me—if you can." A frustrating aspect of Harry's inventions was that he rarely understood how they worked. He was like some drunken chef who never writes down a recipe. This idiosyncrasy of Harry's had prevented Fletcher & Company from getting patents on any of his inventions, and had eventually made people unwilling to contract with us.

"I needed your encouragement, Fletcher. I've come back here to make sure you really are going to see me tomorrow. I remember that when you showed up tomorrow you'd seen me tiny in your car."

This was a very strange mixture of tenses. I thought for a minute, then got the picture. "You mean you're from the future? You've invented time travel?"

The little man on the dashboard glowed with pride. "Time travel's nothing compared to what I'm going to do. I'm master of space and time, Fletch."

I fought back a laugh. Dumpy, rope-lipped Harry, the king of creation? "Do you write that with capital letters, Harry? Master of Space and Time?"

"It's not funny. I could kill you right now if I wanted to. But you're the one who'll give me the idea to build the blunzer. You have to come see me tomorrow. I'll be at the shop. Tomorrow we get the parts, and Sunday night we build the machine."

"I suppose you want money?" I looked around the car, expecting to spot a holocaster. This had to be some kind of trick.

"Money? As I recall, you took two thousand out of your bank account. And you can stop looking around like that, Fletcher. This is for real. I'm master of space and time."

"Prove it. Do something weird. Put me—put me in an infinite regress."

"I knew you'd say that. You're so anal, Fletcher. Too much math. Here, you can light this to get back out."

The little figure tossed something at me. A tiny stick of dynamite, bright red and with a wispy unlit fuse. Something went funny with the time just then; it was like my time line branched right off from reality. Instead of hitting me in the face, the little stick of dynamite just hung there in midair, barely moving. Meanwhile, Harry was shrinking, moving away from me in some unknown dimension. Everything was getting dark and Harry's voice was too faint and high to understand.

Then Harry was all gone, and the world went black, blacker than night, zero photons black. I fumbled around, found the controls, and turned on my headlights. I could see outside, but I couldn't figure out what I was looking at. My car seemed to be resting on black felt, and ahead of the car was a soft, horizontally grooved wall. There was more black cloth to the left of me, and to the right there was a cliff with a big white pole swooping up from its edge. White plastic with sebaceous cracks. The scene made no sense whatsoever.

Although my dome light wasn't on, the inside of my car was lit up. I glanced around to find the cause. Resting on the seat next to me, there was a sort of toy car, a scale-model 1956 Buick with blazing headlights. The headlights were aimed at my corduroy-clad right leg. It looked as if the little car even had a toy driver. I put my hand on it, then drew back with a scream.

Just as my thumb touched the wraparound windshield of the model car, a giant's hand had swooped down out of the darkness to press its hamlike thumb against my own windshield! When I withdrew my hand, the giant followed suit.

I leaned down to peer into the model car's side window. It was lit up in there, too. I could make out a very strange sight. Sitting on the front seat of the model car was a still smaller model car. And peering into the window of the still smaller model was a thumb-sized little copy of me, Joseph Fletcher. The hair on my neck prickled as I realized that, staring in through my own car's window, there must be the eye of a giant Joe Fletcher.

I whirled around, hoping to see the giant's eye, but he turned as fast as I did. All I could see of him was the cheek of his huge head. He had whirled to stare out the window of *his* car, the giant car on whose seat my own car was resting. I could see beyond his cheek and out his window— out there was the head of a yet larger giant, and so on and on, forever up and down. I was embedded in a *doubly* infinite regress. Why on earth had I asked for this? And how had Harry done it? I had to escape!

I flung open my car door, jumped out, and found myself on the seat of the giant's car. When I looked out the giant's car door, I could see the giant, standing on the seat of a yet larger car, and staring out at the yet larger giant. Looking back into my own car, I could see the little model on the seat, and the thumb-sized Fletcher standing next to it and staring back in at the ant-sized Fletcher on the model's seat. No matter how fast I turned, I could never see myself face to face.

I threw myself back into my car and turned on the radio. Static crackled from my speaker and from the endless speakers beyond and within my car. Static, and then a voice, a strangely familiar voice.

"THE RED GLUONS ONLY WORK ONCE," said the radio.

"Hi?" I called questioningly. The giant Fletcher outside roared along, and from the tiny car on the seat came thumb-sized Fletcher's squeak: "Hi?"

"USE BLUE GLUONS THE SECOND TIME."

"What's your name?"

"IT'S A TYPE OF EXCLUSION PRINCIPLE."

"Please help me get out."

"LIGHT THE FUSE."

Silence fell. After a minute I flicked off the radio. Just then something bounced off my cheek. It was the miniature dynamite stick that Harry had thrown at me—how long ago? Time was all messed up.

I picked up the dynamite and struck a match. The larger and smaller Fletchers did the same thing. I lit the fuse and tossed the dynamite out the window. A tiny, tiny version of it flew out the window of the model car on the seat next to me. I braced myself.

The dynamites all blew at once, and I saw stars: cartoon stars and wacky spirals. When the dust settled, I was back where I'd started, at the crazed white plastic steering wheel of my Buick in the Softech parking lot. A square of sunlight lay on my lap, heavy and insistent. I turned the ignition to ON and fired up the big V-8.

2

My American Home

WHEN I pulled into the driveway, my two-year-old daughter Serena was out in the front yard flailing at something with my fishing rod. She was holding the rod by the tip and slamming the reel down on the ground.

"Dada!" she cried. "Wiggle whack crawly bug!" Something moved in the grass, and Serena whipped my rod back for a real knockout punch. The fiberglass snapped, and the piece with the reel flew over to crash on my Buick's shiny hood.

I got out of the car and tried to just walk on past her. I was definitely ripe for my Friday-afternoon beer. But Serena was too fast for me. She put herself between me and the house.

"Bad crawly bug!" She pointed with the tip of my broken rod. "Try bite Serena!"

I gave a heavy sigh and went over to look. Serena was hell on insects. A badly mashed stag beetle was lying in the grass. I was relieved that it wasn't a little Harry.

"Where's Mommy, Serena?"

"Mama lie down."

"Were you a good girl today?"

"Babby bite." She held out her hand to show me a tiny cut on her forefinger.

"The neighbor's baby bit you? What were you doing to it?"

"Playing. Babby bite. Mary Jo wash."

Mary Jo was the name of the woman next door. Serena liked to go over and pick on her baby. "Was Mary Jo mad at you?"

"Mary Jo wash." Serena showed me her finger again. The cut certainly did look clean.

"How nice of Mary Jo to wash your cut. I just hope her baby doesn't have rabies." I patted Serena on the head. She was a brat, but she was mine. "Would you like a candy?"

"Yus."

"Here." I found a linty cough drop in my pants pocket. "Now don't bother that baby any more. And put my fishing rod away."

"Bug gone."

"I'm going inside to see Mommy now, Serena. Be good." I walked into our crummy house, still brooding over Harry's message. There could be money in this, big money.

I found Nancy flaked out on our double bed with a stack of old *People* magazines and an over-flowing ashtray. The TV was going full blast in the other room. I closed the door.

"God, Joey, I have such a backache today. And this morning Serena—"

"Yeah, I've had a rough day myself. Is there any beer?"

"Do you think you could rub my back a little?"

"If you move the ashtray. You know I don't like you to smoke in our bedroom."

"Then why don't you buy a couch for the living room. I hate living like this. We might as well be in a trailer park."

When we'd first married, we'd had a much nicer home. But I'd lost it when Fletcher & Company went bankrupt. The house we rented now was a low-ceilinged three-room tract home: two bedrooms and a kitchen-dining-living room. Looking out the bedroom window, I could see fifty-three houses exactly like ours (one Sunday afternoon I'd counted them). Our development was a reclaimed marsh with woods all around it.

"I'm going to go see Harry tomorrow. I think he's invented something new."

"Don't give him any money, Joseph. I mean it. We need that money for our Christmas trip."

"What trip?"

"Don't you ever listen to anything I tell you?"

"Look, I'm going to get a beer. You want one?"

"How about my back rub?"

Nancy was lying on her stomach. I sat on the backs of her legs and worked my fingers up and down her spine. She felt small and fragile, and she gave off a good smell. My woman.

"I'm sorry to complain so much, Joey. At least we have enough to eat. There's another terrible famine going on in Mexico, did you know?"

Nancy had some strange complexes about food. She was into world hunger, often serving on committees and raising funds. Yet she herself ate very immoderately. Somehow she never seemed to gain weight.

"No, I didn't know that. This afternoon, when I went out to the Buick in the lot, something really—"

Someone was trying to open the bedroom door. Serena.

"Just a minute, sweetie! Does that feel better, Nancy?"

"A little. Could you do something with Serena? She's been just awful. This morning she went next door and stuck her hand in the baby's mouth. That baby only has one tooth, but it bit Serena and she threw a fit. Mary Jo had to carry her back here."

"What a brat."

"Oh, but be nice to her. I was just like Serena when I was little."

Unable to turn the knob, Serena began kicking the door. "Dada! Dada! Dada! Dada!"

"Here I come. Don't break the door."

When I opened the door, Serena squealed and toddled off at high speed. I followed her into the kitchen and popped the top on a Bud. One thing about Nancy, she kept the fridge well-stocked. I inhaled the first beer and started a second. That regress had been bad news. In a way it had taken place outside of time. I wondered what would have happened if I'd wrung the neck of the thumb-sized Fletcher in the toy car. The giant would have done the same to me, of course, while being choked himself and uh uh uh. Hall of mirrors. Harry's doing. Master of space and time. I'd ask him for five million.

I got out the phone book and looked under *Appliances, Service and Repair.* Harry had taken over his family's business when his parents died last winter. I'd never seen the place yet. The ad was pure Harry:

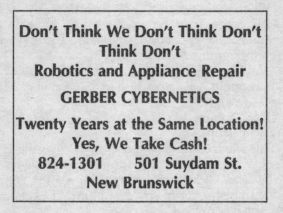

Don't Think We Don't Think Don't Think Don't
Robotics and Appliance Repair

GERBER CYBERNETICS

Twenty Years at the Same Location!
Yes, We Take Cash!
824-1301   501 Suydam St.
New Brunswick

Cybernetics. That was a word Harry and I had always laughed about. Nobody has any idea what it means, it's just some crazy term that Norbert Wiener made up. Gerber Cybernetics. I dialed the number.

"Hello?" An old woman's questioning quaver.

"This is Joseph Fletcher. Is Mr. Gerber in?"

"I'll get him. *Haaaaaaaary!*" There were footsteps, the sound of breaking glass, a curse, some yelling. The person at the other end knocked the phone off the counter, then picked it up.

"Hello?"

"Harry! What do you have?" I lowered my voice

so that Nancy wouldn't hear me. "I can spare two grand, but no more."

"Who's this?" He sounded confused. In the background the old-woman-voice was still yelling.

"*Who's this.* Who do you think it is, space cadet?"

"Is this Joe Fletcher?"

"I'm supposed to come tomorrow, right?"

"We're open ten to five on Saturdays."

"I'll come in early and we can have lunch together. Like real businessmen. Do you have any circuit diagrams for the thing?"

"You want me to invent something?"

"I thought you already had it. *Master of Space and Time,* right?"

"I don't know what you're talking about, Fletch. Are you drunk?"

This was getting nowhere fast. If the little Harrys had been from the future, then maybe he really *didn't* know what I was talking about. "You're going to be master of space and time," I explained. "I want five million dollars."

"Hold on." There were voices in the background. "Yes, it's ready, ma'am. Fletcher, I'm going to have to hang up. Customers. See you tomorrow!"

Serena had climbed onto my lap while I was talking. She was about as short as you can be and still walk. I planted a kiss on her fat little cheek. "You're not really a brat, are you?"

"Dada hand." She starfished her little paw against my palm. "Serena hand!"

I looked around our shabby living area. Everything plastic, piles of laundry, and the TV always on. I wished I'd bought some good furniture when I'd had the money. Nancy and Serena deserved better than this.

3

The Peasant and the Sausage

SATURDAY was cool and rainy. I stopped by my bank and then drove to New Brunswick. Harry's shop was in a crummy neighborhood near the train station. There was a bus station too, and next to it was a place called the Terminal Bar. Some terminal-type guys gimped past in the wet, one of them an obvious wirehead. He was so far gone that he used a mechanical walker. You could see the bulge of his stim-unit under his overcoat.

"Where's Gerber Cybernetics?" I asked. "Man."

"Gug-ger-bub-ber? Ruh-hight thu-there. Man."

The shop had a big plate-glass window, a dirty window crowded with junk: a plastic toad wearing a crown, an old cookie tin with cityscapes embossed on its sides, an out-of-date girlie calendar from the Rigid Tool Company, an oriental lamp, some listless houseplants, a coiled-up orange extension cord, and a terrarium with a mean-looking little lizard in it. I squatted down to get a better look at the lizard. He was like a miniature Godzilla, with powerful rear legs and a long, toothy jaw. He looked as if he'd been in a fight recently, and seemed to be in some pain.

The letters GERBER APPLIANCE arced across the plateglass window, but with the APPLIANCE only a pale, scraped-off shadow. In place of it, crudely brushed in, was the new designation: CYBERNETICS. I opened the door and entered, feeling like a twelve-yearold come to play with his best friend's train set.

The front of the shop was cramped, with a waisthigh counter. A partition behind the counter divided the store from the actual work area in the rear. A robot stood behind the counter, scanning me. It was a multipurpose Q-89, with the small, bullet-shaped head and the long, snaky arms.

"What can we do you for?" The machine was programmed to sound like a friendly old woman. I'd talked to it on the phone.

"I'm Joe Fletcher. Mr. Gerber's expecting me."

"You can call me Antie," said the robot. "A-N-T-I-E. Harry's in back."

"Thank you, Antie."

She—with the voice you had to think of Antie as female—stepped aside and I went through the door behind the counter. It was a regular workshop back there, with shelves of parts, a wall of tools, and a number of partially disassembled electronic devices. The resinous tang of solder smoke perfumed the air. I felt right at home.

Harry looked up from a robot torso and gave me a big smile. "Fletcher! It's been a long time."

"I've been busy with the job and the wife, Harry. Great to see you." I looked around the crowded workroom. "So this is the Gerber family business, eh? You making any money?"

"Yeah, some. But it's boring. I'm all alone here except for Antie."

"Why does she talk like an old woman?"

"My mom did that. She programmed Antie to talk and act just like her . . . before she died. I keep meaning to change it, but I don't know, it's sort of soothing." Harry sighed and laid down his soldering ray. "But what was that phone call of yours all about? Master of space and time?"

Before I could really start, Antie interrupted.

"Would you like some soup, Dr. Fletcher?" The robot shuffled into the room, bearing a tray with two steaming bowls of thick, dark lentil soup.

"Well . . . I'd really been planning to take Harry out for lunch."

"You two can still go out. It won't hurt my feelings. I'm just a machine. Should I put some quark in that, boys?"

"Quark?" I inquired.

"Quark," confirmed Harry with a chuckle. "But not the particle. *Quark* is a German word for a kind of yogurt. My family always used it to mean *sour cream*. That's a big Hungarian thing, you know, lentil soup with sour cream. Try it, it's delicious."

"Okay."

Antie served us our soup with quark and, at Harry's urging, went out to the Terminal Bar for some Utz pretzels and Blatz beer. I gave Harry a detailed account of my experiences of the day before. He was particularly interested in the fact that when he traveled back in time, he'd only looked two inches tall to me.

"So Fred Hoyle was right," Harry exclaimed. "Everything is shrinking!"

"Nothing's shrinking, Harry. I'm the same size every day."

"That's what you *think*. But your house shrinks, your car shrinks, your wife shrinks—everything in the universe is shrinking at the same rate. That's why the distant galaxies keep seeming farther away. I'd always wondered how to test it. But now—"

"Time travel!" I exclaimed. "I get it. If everything's smaller now than it was yesterday, then if I jump back through time to yesterday, I'm much smaller than the people there."

"That's it, Fletch. That's why the time-traveling Harry you saw yesterday was so small. He was from the future. And the other way would be the opposite."

"You mean that if we could jump something a few days forward in time it would come out seeming huge?"

"Yeah." Harry beamed at me for a second. We were having fun. "You say I called the machine a blunzer?"

"That's right. A blunzer. You said we built it and it made you master of space and time."

"Blunzer . . . I like that. Did I say when we built it? Or how?"

"We build it tomorrow, and today we get the parts. You said that if I came to see you today, you'd know what to do. The very fact that you were able to come back from the future means that the blunzer is going to work, right?"

"Well, yes. The idea of controlling space and time does happen to be something I've been thinking about recently. The way I see it, it's simply a matter of increasing the value of Planck's constant by many orders of magnitude."

"That's what you've been working on?"

"After a fashion." Harry smiled lopsidedly and fell silent. I realized then that he'd been unable to work without me. It had been a shame to let Nancy come between us.

"Have you done any experiments?"

"No, I didn't have the energy. This is all so strange. First I have some ideas, then the ideas decide to become real. The blunzer sends me back in time to get you to help me build the blunzer. It's a closed causal loop. But where did it come from?"

"God, maybe. Or another dimension. You're telling me you actually know how to build the blunzer?"

"I had a dream about it last night, as a matter of fact. I dreamed that you were explaining it to me. It was a very vivid dream." Harry stared into space, thinking. "The materials are going to cost," he said finally. "You only brought two thousand dollars?"

"It's all I have. I work and work and the savings never grow. It's horrible to have a real job, Harry, they treat me just like anyone else. I'm ready to gamble everything on you."

"Well, thanks, Fletch. I'm really touched. With you helping me, the blunzer might work. Planck's constant, you know, it's a measure of the effect that the observer has on the universe. If I can temporarily increase the value of Planck's constant in my body, then the world will look more and more like I want it to."

"Here's the beer, boys." Antie came shuffling back from her run.

We each opened a can. I drank deep and sighed with pleasure. "Drinking beer in a back room on a rainy Saturday. This is the life, Harry, with no women around. Nancy and Serena—"

"It's rough, huh? Well, living alone gets pretty old, too."

"Do you have any girl friends?"

"There's one woman I've been seeing. She's a student at the Scientific Mysticism Seminary here. Kind of plain, but very pleasant. She slept here last night. I just wish I could get her to stop talking about God."

"What's her name?"

"Sondra Tupperware. Sondra with an *o*."

I burst out laughing. The name was too ridiculous to be believed. "You lying toad. Has anything you've told me yet been true?"

"It's *all* true. You're the one who saw me come back from the future."

"Nobody's called Tupperware."

"You want to phone her up?"

"I'll have another beer instead. Tell me more about what you think the blunzer will do."

"We'll talk about the technical details later. The main thing is that it'll make me master of space and time. For a while, anyway. Whatever I wish for will come true."

"And me? Do I get a turn?"

"Sure. First I'll do it, then you."

"That'll be safer," I observed. "So I can undo anything you screw up too badly."

"Like 'The Peasant and the Sausage,' " said Harry. "You know that story?"

"No."

"Well, there's a peasant who finds a little man trapped in a bramble bush. He gets the little man out, and the little man says, 'In return for your help I grant you three wishes. Use them wisely!' So the peasant runs home and talks it over with his wife. They're trying to decide what to wish for. They're talking and talking and suppertime comes, and she's been too busy to fix anything, and she's real hungry. 'I wish I had a nice big sausage,' the wife blurts out, and there on the table in front of her is a crisp white bratwurst. 'God, you're stupid!' the husband shouts, beside himself with rage. 'I wish that sausage would grow onto your nose!' So there's the poor wife with the big gross sausage grown onto her face."

"And they have to use the third wish to get the sausage off, right?"

"Yeah. Three wishes and all they end up with is a sausage."

"But the blunzer gives you more than three wishes, doesn't it?"

"It gives all the wishes I make, but only for a limited period of time. A session with the blunzer is like one super-wish."

"Couldn't you wish for infinitely many wishes?"

"I don't think so. You have to wish for something concrete."

"So what are you going to wish for, Harry?"

Harry smiled and rubbed his face. "That's the

hard part, isn't it? I'll get you some money—I know you'll want that, and—"

"That's right," I put in. "Five million bucks."

"Yeah. And I wish Sondra was prettier. And I wish the blunzer would work. And . . . I don't know. I'd like to have some big adventure happen. Subconscious wishes count too, which means that—"

"Try to do the big adventure in some other universe," I suggested. "So this one doesn't get totally wrecked."

"That sounds like a good idea. I'll wish for a magic door to another world and we can go over there for a while."

"Hey, I'm psyched, Harry!"

"Let's go shopping."

4

Stars 'n' Bars

W^E left Antie in charge of the store and took off in my Buick. Without Harry having to tell me, I knew where we were headed. Jack McCormack's Stars 'n' Bars Government Surplus.

Harry handed me a pretzel and an open beer. "Utz and Blatz, Fletcher, just think about it."

"Tzzzz."

We were on an incredibly built-up divided highway. There were lots of potholes. The traffic was light but intense. The government had recently repealed all speed limits in an attempt to boost oil consumption.

Businesses were slotted in side by side, not only along both edges of the highway but also all up and down the broad median strip. Such dense social tissue needs a vast traffic flow to nourish it, a flow that was no longer available in these depression times. Many of the businesses stood empty. Fly-by-night operations flitted in and out of the abandoned rent-free shells like fish in a coral reef.

COSMO FLEXADYNE!

PERSONA SCREAM-FLASH!

BLOOD AND ORGANS BOUGHT AND SOLD!

FETISH MEGAMART!

ETHICAL REPROGRAMMING!

FLESH FISH!

NORTH JERSEY'S ONLY DOG BUTCHER!

EXCRETION THERAPY!

SKIN SHIRTS—WE MAKE OR EAT!

BAG BODY BOXING!

STARS 'N' BARS SURPLUS!

"There it is."

We pulled into the vast empty lot of what had once been a Two Guys discount center. The building was a weathered yellow cube with half an American flag painted on one side. A few robots loitered outside the entrance, standing guard. Jack McCormack, the proprietor, was a displaced redneck, deeply suspicious of city folks.

When we pulled up, Jack had been standing behind the glass doors, watching the traffic. But when he saw Harry and me, he turned and disappeared into the gloomy recesses of his domain.

"Plllease state youuur business," intoned one of the robots, a squat K-88 with a flare ray bolted to its arm.

"Joseph Fletcher and Harry Gerber, out shopping. Jack knows us."

"Nnnnnegatory. You willl leave the area."

"Come on, McCormack," shouted Harry, "you remember us. We built that beam weapon for

General Moritz. The thing to make water radioactive?" That had been one of our less successful designs. Harry had lost the plans for the demonstration model, and we'd been unable to duplicate it.

"Nnnnnegatory," hummed the robot, leveling its flare ray. "Therrre willl be no furrrtherrr warnings." The flare ray looked truly vicious: it was something like a small industrial laser with a superheterodyne unit in back.

"We've got *cash*!" I screamed. "Two thousand dollars!"

"Well, why dintcha say so?" At the mention of money, the robot's speaker switched from taped threats to McCormack's lively drawl. The machine scurried to open the glass doors. "Y'all boys still owes Stars 'n' Bars right much."

"That's right," I confessed. "Five hundred dollars, wasn't it?"

"Hot golly, les call it three!" Jack McCormack stepped forward from behind some giant spools of cable. "Assumin y'all boys is really goan spend two kay." He was a leathery little gnome with hard blue eyes.

"Oh, we'll spend more than that," said Harry breezily. "Though you should realize, McCormack, that Fletcher & Company qualified for the Emergency Bankruptcy Act of '95, so that any debts or obligations of the aforesaid corporation are void."

"Yew fat ugly toad. Ah bet yore foreign, ain't yew?"

"Hungarian-American. And, unlike you, with a full command of the English language."

Looking at the two short men glaring at each other, one fat, one skinny, I had to laugh. "Look,

Jack." I took out my wallet. "Real cash. Get the truck."

McCormack had a small pickup that you could drive around his huge store. The three of us piled in, me in the middle.

"First we need a hotshot table," said Harry.

"Good God!" I exclaimed. "Whatever for?" The hotshot table had been a popular execution device during the early nineties, when capital punishment had made a big comeback. A hotshot table was like a hospital gurney, a bed on wheels, but a bed with certain built-in servo-mechanisms. It was a kind of mechanical Dr. Death, equipped to give fatal brain injections to condemned criminals. Lying down on a hotshot table was like lying down on a black widow's belly. The needle would stab right down into the top of your head. The point of the thing was that it had helped resolve the AMA's scruples about helping to kill people. But now capital punishment had been voted out again.

"That's aw-reet," McCormack was saying. "We got 'em in stock. New or used? Used costs extry—people buy 'em for parties, like."

"Good God! A new one!"

"Got me one still in the crate. Over on aisle naaane." Great mounds of machinery slid past, lit by our little truck's headlights. Some heavy robots pounded along behind us, ready to help with the loading.

"A large vacuum pump," said Harry. "And a walk-in refrigerator."

"Kin do, kin do."

"Thirty square meters of copper foil."

"Uh-huh."

"A mater-driven microwave cavity."

"Got one on sale."

The truck darted this way and that.

"A vortex coil," said Harry. "And two meters of sub-ether wave guide."

"Yowzah!"

"And the key ingredient—a magnetic bottle with two hundred grams of red gluons!"

"Great day in the mornin'!"

"And that'll do it."

"Don't he beat all?" McCormack asked me. "Some of these bohunks is smart, and that's no lie."

Before too long we had everything hauled to the front of the store. McCormack fiddled with his calculator. "Ah make it tin thousand dollar."

"Get serious."

"It's them gluons. They're high, even in red."

"Pay him," Harry urged. "Once I get blunzed, we'll have it all."

"Blunzed?" inquired McCormack, glancing at Harry.

"Once I get blunzed I'll be able to control reality," Harry explained. "I'll get you all the money you want."

"Ah don't want *all* the money. Ah want tin thousand dollar."

"Uh, I have two thousand in cash, Mr. McCormack. Can I give you a check for the rest?"

McCormack threw back his head and laughed. There were cords in his skinny neck.

"How would you like to be a partner?" I suggested. "We'll issue you some shares of stock."

McCormack laughed harder. It wasn't really a pleasant sound.

Harry had been off to one side, looking over our intended purchases, but now he rejoined me. "Let's go out to the car for a minute, Fletcher. I just thought of something."

"Ah hope ah din't haul all this gear up front for nothin'!" complained McCormack.

"We'll be right back," Harry assured him. "I believe we've got some more money out in the car."

McCormack's guard robots followed us out to my Buick. "You left money out here?" I asked Harry. "Why didn't you tell me?"

"Well, it just now occurred to me that I might have. When I came back from the future to your car yesterday, I could have created money and put it under your seat. It would be the obvious thing to do, right?"

I got the door unlocked and reached under the driver's seat. Sure enough, a dense wad of bills: eight thousand dollars' worth, exactly what we needed.

"If these are from the future, then why aren't they real small?" I asked Harry. "Like *you* were."

"I made them the right size, is all. It's obvious. Master of space and time!"

I stared at him for a long time. "Why couldn't you create the whole ten thousand? Why make me put up my only two?"

"You offered your money of your own free will, Fletch. You're in this, too."

I sighed and took all our money in to Jack McCormack. "Ten thousand, right?"

"Tin thousand and the three hunnert from before."

Suddenly I lost my temper. The fact that I'd had eight thousand bucks in my car without knowing it really got to me.

"The deal's off, Jack." I turned to leave. I had an overwhelming urge to take the money back to Nancy and forget about these little guys.

"Hey now," McCormack cried. "Y'all kin still owe me that five hunnert. And tell you whut. Ah'll truck yore goods home free."

"Give him the money, Fletch. Bring it to 501 Suydam, McCormack. Gerber Cybernetics. There's an alley in back."

5

Godzilla Meets the Toad Man

"LET'S take the Jersey Turnpike home," suggested Harry. "It's faster."

"Okay. And give me another beer." I was feeling happy again. "This blunzer is really going to work. I mean, here you've already traveled back in time and created eight thousand dollars. It's fantastic."

"One thing about time travel," said Harry musingly. "There probably has to be a counterweight. Action equals reaction, you know."

"What do you mean?"

"I mean that if I travel from the future to the past, then something has to travel from the past to the future. To balance things out. When I jump back to Friday afternoon, I'll probably have to jump some organism forward a few days."

"If you jump an animal forward, it'll seem real big," I reminded Harry.

"That's right. Every object in the universe is shrinking, so if something jumps forward a few days it seems enormous. Did you ever see any Godzilla movies, Fletch? With the giant lizard?"

I shot a look over at Harry. His expression was bland and unreadable. I started to say something, then let it drop. He was just trying to get a rise out of me.

The Jersey Turnpike's pavement was in good repair today. A Porsche passed us, doing what looked like 120 miles per hour. Its tires threw up a long, blinding shock-cone of rainwater. I stuck to the slow lane and kept my eyes open. To the right were the refineries, to the left were docks and railyards.

Harry powered down his window and inhaled deeply. "Ah! *This* is the smell of American richness."

Many years ago Fletcher & Company had done some business designing stack scrubbers for one of these companies. But now times were so hard that nobody much cared about pollution. The main thing was just to keep the factories open. As long as they stank, you knew they weren't idle.

Although I couldn't share Harry's pleasure at the unearthly smells, this stretch of the Jersey Turnpike was one of my favorite places. I was particularly fond of the refinery cracking towers, those great abstract totems of knotted pipe and wire. And the big storage tanks, the code-painted conduits, the webs of scaffolding, the catwalks, the great pulsing gas flares—all sheerly functional, yet charged with surreal meaning. I felt like a cockroach in a pharmacy.

"What is that over there?" said Harry, interrupting my reverie. "Do you hear that noise?"

There was a deep, spasmodic roaring coming from the direction of the docks. The sound grew louder, and now you could hear sirens as well, sirens and gunshots. I slowed down a bit, and Harry and I peered off to the left. There was something big there, an immense shadowy form, *a giant lizard stomping a warehouse*. Crashes and roars. A boxcar went flying. A high-tension electrical tower crumpled and great sparks flew.

I stepped on the gas, but Harry reached over and took the key out of the ignition.

"Stop!" he commanded. "I want to enjoy this!"

I had no choice but to pull off into the emergency lane. Some other rubberneckers had already done the same. Just a few hundred meters off was a huge predatory lizard, a two-hundred-foot Godzilla with a head like a man-eating garbage scow. One of the refinery's gas flares pulsed up just then, and the monster threw back his head to roar defiance.

GWEEEEEEEEEENT! AH-ROOOOOOOOO-OOOOOONKH!

A police car pulled up on the side of the turnpike and one of the cops opened up on the monster with a heavy machine gun.

Budda-ba-budda-burrtttt!

RRRAAAAAAANH! RRWAAAAAAAAAEEE-EEEEEE!

Budda-burrtttt-brrt!

RRRRWWOOOOOOOOOOOOOOOOO!

The ground shook as the monster charged.

I was yelling, yelling at Harry. "Goddamnit,

Harry, I know this is your fault! You jumped a lizard up in time! Give me those keys before—"

"Shut up, Fletcher. I've always wanted to have Godzilla real. The noise!"

The police car flew into the air and crashed, burning, on the roadway nearby.

FWWWWWUUUUUEEEEE! WWREEEEEEE-EENH!

"Good God, he's headed for us! He knows you, Harry! Let's get out of here!"

Harry was too enraptured to recognize our danger. I bundled him down the highway embankment. At the bottom was a culvert, a four-foot cement pipe running right under the turnpike.

"In here!"

GUH-WHEEEEEEEENT! REEEEEEEENTH-REEEEEEEENT-REEEEEEEEEENT!

The giant lizard was really getting excited. And—God, God, God—it was Harry and me he was after. We barely made it into the culvert in time. A huge claw probed in after us, and was replaced by the creature's immense basilisk eye.

"Isn't this exciting, Fletch? Watch this!"

Harry yelled and threw a sharp rock right into the giant eye's center.

WHEEEENK-WHEEEENK-WHEEEENK! GUH-ROOOOOOOOOOOOOOOOOO!

"I love that noise," chortled Harry. "I can't get enough of it."

The monster's huge claws were tearing at the culvert's end. Meters of sod crumbled and great chunks of concrete flew. Our tunnel grew steadily shorter. Harry was looking around for another rock to throw.

"Oh, God, Harry, I hate you so much, you crazy wrecked slob, you don't care about anything real! Oh, Nancy, I'm so sorry I got involved! Please, God, help me, save me, save me—"

A third of our tunnel was gone now. The Godzilla-thing had us trapped like rats. The only escape was to run out the other end. I took off, leaving Harry behind. He was laughing and hefting a rock. Was he nuts, or did he know something I didn't know.

It was marshy on the other side of the turnpike, too marshy to head off overland. The only way out was along the roadway itself.

The giant lizard was concentrating on its digging—there hadn't been any roaring for several minutes. Gathering my courage, I crawled up the embankment to peer back across the turnpike.

There was the monster's great lashing tail, and there, twenty meters off to the left, was my car, still unharmed.

"Oh, Nancy," I moaned, "I'm coming, baby."

I sprinted across the northbound lanes and the median. Every hair on my neck was standing up. I got back into my Buick. Harry had left the key on the seat. I fumbled it into the ignition and started . . .

ROOOOOOOOOOOOOOOOOOOOONT! SQUAA-ROOOOOOOONT-ROOOOOONT-ROOOOO-OOOONT!

Harry had just thrown his second rock. Forget it, man, and color me gone. I floored the accelerator and peeled out. I was still shaking when I pulled into my driveway back in Princeton.

6

The Central Teachings of Mysticism

Nancy was at the kitchen table, eating a dish of yogurt with Froot Loops. The TV was on full blast. A quiz show. Serena was lying on her side, sucking the corner of a blanket.

"Couldn't you turn down the TV?" I demanded.

"Mr. Big Shot," muttered Nancy, not taking her eyes off the screen. All the chairs had piles of laundry on them, so I flopped down on the floor next to Serena.

"What's the matter, Nancy?"

"You," she said. Her eyes were red and puffy. She'd been crying. Her head kept jerking the way it always did when she was really mad at me. "You gave all our money to your crazy friend, didn't you? I wanted to go shopping, and the bank said we've got nothing left. Mr. Big Deal."

She ripped open a package of Oreos and started

eating the cookies two at a time. I could never understand where Nancy put all the food she ate. Someone on TV won a prize. The audience roared like a broken washing machine. Serena sucked on her blanket, staring blankly at the tube.

"I'm sorry, Nancy. You're right, I gave our money to Harry. And I shouldn't have. He's not to be trusted. Did you hear the news yet? A giant lizard almost killed me on the Jersey Turnpike?"

Nancy stubbed her cigarette out in the overflowing ashtray, and lit another, chewing all the while. She tilted her head back to keep the smoke out of her eyes. "All I can say, Joseph, is that—is that . . ." Abruptly she burst into sobs.

I got up and put my arm around her. I took the cigarette out of her mouth and put my cheek against hers. My frail strawberry-blond darling. My southern belle. "I—I did it for you, Nancy! I want us to be rich and happy again."

"No!" She pushed me away, knocking her ashtray off the table. It shattered on the floor. Ashes and broken glass. Serena scrambled over to investigate.

"Look out, Serena, there's broken glass. Let Daddy clean it up."

Nancy and Serena watched me clean up the mess. I used a paper towel and piece of the Froot Loops box. At the end I cut my finger, probably on purpose. "Damn. Oh damn, damn, damn."

Sunday morning we went to church, the First Church of Scientific Mysticism. The religion, vaguely Christian, had grown out of the mystical teachings of Albert Einstein and Kurt Gödel, the two great Princeton sages. Nancy and I didn't attend regularly, but today it seemed like the thing to do. According to the evening news, Godzilla had suddenly disappeared after digging a trench across the Jersey Turnpike. The news didn't mention if Harry had escaped, but it stood to reason that he had. I guess I was glad.

The sun was out, and the three of us had a nice time walking over to church.

"I'm sorry I was so ugly to you yesterday, Joe."

"And I'm sorry about the money, baby. Maybe we can drive up to New Brunswick today and see what Harry's done with it."

"No, thanks." Nancy looked light and pretty in her Sunday dress. I took her hand. Serena skipped along ahead of us, light as dandelion fluff.

The church building was a remodeled bank, a massive granite building with big pillars and heavy bronze lamps. Inside, there were pews and a raised pulpit. In place of an altar was a large hologram of Albert Einstein. Einstein smiled kindly, occasionally blinking his eyes. Nancy and Serena and I took a pew halfway up the left side. The organist was playing a Bach prelude. I gave Nancy's hand a squeeze. She squeezed back.

Today's service was special. The minister, an elderly physicist named Alwin Bitter, was celebrating the installation of a new assistant, a woman named—*Sondra Tupperware.* I jumped when I heard her name, remembering that Harry had mentioned her yesterday. Was this another of his fantasies become real? Yet Ms. Tupperware looked solid enough: a skinny woman with red glasses-frames and a springer spaniel's kinky brown hair.

Old Bitter was wearing a tuxedo with a thin pink necktie. The dark suit set off his halo of white hair to advantage. He passed out some bread and wine, and then he gave a sermon called "The Central Teachings of Mysticism."

His teachings, as best I recall, were three in number: (1) All is One; (2) The One is Unknowable; and (3) The One is Right Here. Bitter delivered his truths with a light touch, and the congregation laughed a lot—happy, surprised laughter.

Nancy and I lingered after the service, chatting with some of the church members we knew. I was waiting for a chance to ask Alwin Bitter for some advice.

Finally everyone was gone except for Bitter and Sondra Tupperware. The party in honor of her installation was going to be later that afternoon.

"Is Tupperware your real name?" asked Nancy.

Sondra laughed and nodded her head. Her eyes were big and round behind the red glasses. "My parents were hippies. They changed the family name to Tupperware to get out from under some legal trouble. Dad was a close friend of Alwin's."

"That's right," said Bitter. "Sondra's like a niece to me. Did you enjoy the sermon?"

"It was great," I said. "Though I'd expected more science."

"What's your field?" asked Bitter.

"Well, I studied mathematics, but now I'm mainly in computers. I had my own business for a while. Fletcher & Company."

"You're Joe Fletcher?" exclaimed Sondra. "I know a friend of yours."

"Harry Gerber, right? That's what I wanted to ask Dr. Bitter about. Harry's trying to build something that will turn him into God."

Bitter looked doubtful. I kept talking. "I know it sounds crazy, but I'm really serious. Didn't you hear about the giant lizard yesterday?"

"On the Jersey Turnpike," said Nancy loyally. "It was on the news."

"Yes, but I don't quite see—"

"Harry made the lizard happen. The thing he built—it's called a blunzer—is going to give him control over space and time, even the past. The weird thing is that it isn't really even Harry. The blunzer is just *using* us to make things happen. It sent Harry to tell me to tell Harry to get me to—"

Bitter was looking at his watch. "If you have a specific question, Mr. Fletcher, I'd be happy to answer it. Otherwise . . ."

What *was* my question?

"My question. Okay, it's this: What if a person becomes the same as the One? What if a person can control all of reality? What should he ask for? What changes should he make?"

Bitter stared at me in silence for almost a full minute. I seemed finally to have engaged his imagination. "You're probably wondering why that question should boggle my mind," he said at last. "I wish I could answer it. You ask me to suppose that some person becomes like God. Very well. Now we are wondering about God's motives. Why is the universe the way it is? Could it be any different? What does God have in mind when He makes the world?" Bitter paused and rubbed his eyes. "Can the One really be said to have a mind at all? To have a mind—this means to *want* something. To have *plans*. But wants and plans are partial and relative. The One is absolute. As long as wishes and needs are present, an individual falls short of the final union." Bitter patted my shoulder and gave me a kind look. "With all this said, I urge you to remember that individual existence is in fact identical with the very act of falling short of the final union. Treasure your humanity, it's all you have."

"But—"

Bitter raised his hand for silence. "A related point: There is no one you. An individual is a bundle of conflicting desires, a society in microcosm. Even if some limited individual were seemingly to take control of our universe, the world would remain as confusing as ever. If *I* were to create a world, for instance, I doubt if it would be any different from the one in which we find ourselves." Bitter took my hand and shook it. "And now, if you'll excuse me, I've got to get home for Sunday dinner. Big family reunion today. My wife Sybil's out at the airport picking up our oldest daughter. She's been visiting her grandparents in Germany."

Bitter shook hands with the others and took off, leaving the four of us on the church steps.

"What'd he say?" I asked Sondra.

Sondra shook her head quizzically. Her long, frizzed hair flew out to the sides. "The bottom line is that he wants to have lunch with his family. But tell me more about Harry's project."

"How well do you know Harry?" put in Nancy.

"We've been seeing each other off and on for about six months. He introduced himself to me at the Vienna Café. It's a nice bar and grill in New Brunswick."

"He's no good," said Nancy emphatically. "You

should steer clear of him, Sondra. Do you know what he said when I told him about world hunger? He said, 'There's too damn many people anyway.' Isn't that horrible? And what was it he said at Serena's christening, Joe? Something about dying?"

" 'Born to die' is what he said: 'Fletcher, you've just made something else that has to die.' I know it sounds bad, but there is a certain point to it. If there were no more people, there'd be no more suffering." I was trying to sound as cool as Alwin Bitter. "We want to be alive. Fine. But that means we have to accept the suffering that comes along with living. Don't you agree, Sondra?"

"I'm all for accepting reality," said Sondra with a laugh. "Though I'm not sure that Harry is. Were you serious when you said that he was building a machine to give him control over the universe? Harry Gerber? I *love* Harry, Joe, but—"

For the first time I really let myself imagine the kind of world that Harry might design. The guy had no respect for the ordinary human things that make life worth living. Weirdness was all he cared about. Weirdness and sex and plenty to drink.

"I better go up to New Brunswick," I said abruptly. "Before he gets carried away."

"I didn't mean, *Is it a good idea?*" said Sondra. "I meant, *Do you seriously believe it's possible?* After all, Harry's just a TV repairman. There's a big step from that to—"

"Go, Joey," Nancy urged. "Before it's too late."

"This is getting awfully hysterical," said Sondra. For such a plain woman, she had extraordinary presence. "Maybe I better come along."

"You've got your reception to go to," I reminded her. "And by the way, welcome to our church."

"Yes," said Nancy, "we've been meaning to come more often. But are you going back to New Brunswick after the party, Sondra?"

"Yes."

"Well, stop in at Harry's shop then and make sure Joe's on his way home. When he and Harry start working on something, they lose all track of time. Maybe there isn't any big danger, but still—"

"I'll check up on them, Nancy."

"Thanks."

Nancy and I strolled home together, each of us holding one of Serena's hands. She liked us to swing her in the air. Nancy didn't say much—I could tell she was doing some thinking.

"If it works," she said after a while, "if it works, what are you going to ask for?"

"Five million dollars."

"And for me?"

"What do you mean? The money's for both of us."

"I want more than money. I want you to make a wish for me."

"All right. What do you want?"

"Make Harry eliminate world hunger. Make him come up with something that turns dirt into food." Nancy smiled happily at the thought. "That'll show him!"

7

100,000,000,000,000,000,000,000,000,000, 000,000,000

Harry's shop was locked tight. I pounded and pounded, but nobody came, not even Antie. I decided to try in back. There was a two-story wooden porch. Harry was sitting on the steps in the afternoon sun. He was wearing pajamas and looking through a stack of dirty magazines.

"Hey, Harry!"

"Say, Fletch. You're in time for lunch. Antie's stewing some chicken and my pet lizard, Zeke. He got some wounds and today he died." Harry gave me one of his wet, unfocused smiles.

"The lizard!" I yelped. "I saw him in your store window yesterday! Was he the—"

"That's right. Tonight, when I go back to visit you on Friday, Zeke will jump forward from Thursday to visit you on Saturday. Fifty-five hours each way, with the visits lasting about fifteen minutes. It

43

balances out. I noticed the marks on Zeke when I fed him Thursday, but of course I didn't realize. He was all shot up, poor thing. Antie found lots of little bullets in him when she skinned him today."

"You're lucky you weren't killed yesterday."

"If I'd gotten killed, then it couldn't have happened, could it? Poor Zeke. I'm sorry I threw those rocks at him. But the noise was just so—"

"Harry, I don't think this should go any further. I know that there'll be a time paradox if we don't build the blunzer today, but after seeing what you did yesterday, I'd almost rather—"

"Aw, come on, Fletch. Don't be so—"

"I was talking about it this morning with Nancy and Sondra."

"Sondra Tupperware?"

"She was at our church today, the First Church of Scientific Mysticism. She's the new assistant."

"Oh, yeah, she told me about that. I think mysticism's a bunch of crap. All regions are a bunch of crap."

"What *do* you believe in, Harry?"

"Who's asking?"

"Well, Nancy and Sondra and I were talking, and I realized how disastrous it could be for someone like you to get any kind of control over the world. Do you remember what you said to Nancy when she was talking about world hunger?"

"Sure. 'There's too damn many people anyway.' It's true, Fletcher, and you know it. Don't give me this holier-than-thou routine."

"Are you going to bring some terrible plague down on us, Harry? Would you kill off the whole human race?"

"I'd save *these* girls." Harry grinned and patted his stack of magazines.

"Dinner's ready," called Antie from inside the house.

The whole floor above Harry's shop was an apartment. Apparently Antie had been expecting me; two places were set in the dark old dining room. Harry and I took our seats, and Antie brought in the meal.

Besides the lizard stew, we had fried potatoes, cucumber salad, fresh rolls, a plate of hot sauerkraut, and a bottle of good red wine. Harry ate with his hands.

"The lizard's not bad," I observed between forkfuls. The meat was pale and spongy, a bit like soft-shelled lobster. It gave me a good feeling to be eating something that had tried to kill me only the day before.

"Mmmpf," said Harry by way of agreement. He chewed with his mouth open, then swallowed. "I've always had a thing about Godzilla. It's no surprise I picked on poor Zeke for the counterweight."

"But that's just so irresponsible, Harry. You could have used a *shoe* or something, and then yesterday would have been no problem. A giant shoe would have blocked our way for a while, and then it would have disappeared. How do I know what other craziness you're going to pull? What if you crack the Earth in half or something? You're not into disaster movies, are you?"

"Nah, not really. I got enough of that stuff when I was little. My Dad used to read the Book of Revelations to us every night."

"Oh, brother. That's all we need. Look, Harry,

it's time we had a serious talk. I've seen both you and Zeke travel through time, so I know the blunzer is going to work. We're going to build it today and tonight you'll be master of space and time, at least for a while. God knows I would have picked someone else, but at least you're my friend and I can count on you to make me rich while you have the power, right?"

"No problem. You want gold, or what?"

"Gold's too high profile. Give me five million bucks in paper currency. Used bills, small denominations."

"Okay. What else?"

"Well—this is Nancy's idea. She wants you to make something that will turn dirt into food. A machine or something that's simple to reproduce and—"

"No more world hunger," said Harry expansively. "Fine by me. If I can do it, I will. Let's go downstairs."

"One last thing. All that money isn't going to do me any good if you turn the solar system into cheese or something."

"I don't like cheese."

"You know what I mean, Harry. The blunzer's effects have to be self-limiting. It has to stop working after an hour or two. And then everything has to go back to the way it was."

"Back to the way it was? You don't want your money to disappear, do you? Or Nancy's cure for world hunger?"

"Make a few reasonable changes in our world, fine. And then let's go over to an alternate universe, like I said yesterday. First you do the jump to

Friday, and make the money and everything, and then we go over to another world so you can work out without wrecking things here."

"That sounds good. As long as I'm master of space and time I'll be able to hold open a magic door to the world of my heart's desire. We'll stay two hours and then come back here just before the blunzing wears off. As soon as it wears off, the magic door'll close, and we'll be free to enjoy the few changes I made here."

"Well"—I hesitated, still worrying—"it sounds pretty reasonable. But what if one of the changes you make in our world turns out to be really lethal? If we don't realize till after the blunzing wears off, we'll be stuck with it."

"No we won't. We'll only use up half of those red gluons, so there'll be enough for you to get blunzed and fix everything."

"Like a second wish."

"Sure. 'The Peasant and the Sausage.'"

"Then I guess we've got an agreement."

"How do you know I'll stick to it?" Harry gave me one of his horrible smiles.

"Do I have a choice?"

"You worry too much, Fletch. Come on, let's get started."

Jack McCormack had delivered the goods. The stuff was all in Harry's workshop, stacked by the back door.

"Here's the basic idea," said Harry, slowly pacing back and forth. "We put the hotshot table in the fridge and I lie on it. It's cold in there, and we've got it electromagnetically isolated with the copper foil. Just before I get the injection, the chamber is flash-pumped to vacuum. I'll have an air tank, so no problem."

"No problem? What about the shot? What kind of shot do you get? What happens to you then?"

"Planck juice. I get blunzed." Two made-up words. Harry was flying.

"*Blunzed* I've heard, Harry. But what's this *Planck juice*?"

"Okay. That's going to be your and Antie's job. The idea is that you get Antie to pour half the gluons out of the magnetic bottle and into the microwave cavity. It makes a super-quantum fluid, right?"

"I guess."

"Do you know what gluons *are*, Fletcher?"

"Well, they're real small. They have something to do with quarks."

"Gluons are the particles that stick quarks together. A proton is three quarks with some gluons in there holding the quarks together. The gluons come in three colors: red, blue and yellow. Red are easiest to get."

"Fine. You've got gluons mixed with microwaves to make a super-quantum fluid. Then what?"

"The fluid is guided into the vortex coil."

"The vortex coil!" This was getting exciting.

"The vortex coil. Think of a food processor, Fletch. The super-quantum fluid plops into the vortex coil and *skaaaaazzt!*"

"It's blended."

"Blended into Planck juice, Fletcher, Planck juice being a continuous pre-quark force-medium with no distinguishing characteristic features whatsoever.

It doesn't know what the value of Planck's constant is supposed to be."

"It doesn't know."

"But I'll tell it! I'll lie to it! The first thing I'll show the Planck juice will be a one-meter tunnel of wave guide! So the Planck length will seem like one meter instead of 10^{-33} centimeters! That's a hundred-decillion-fold amplification, Fletcher!"

"Harry, I don't know what you're talking about."

"The Planck length is the size level at which quantum uncertainty takes over. The Planck juice will be manipulated into behaving as if the Planck length were one meter. And I'll absorb the juice. What the blunzer is going to do for me is to greatly magnify the uncertainty around me. Things will do what I tell them to!"

"Let's backtrack a little, Harry. We've got the Planck juice in the wave guide now. The wave guide takes it to the hotshot table, which injects it into your brain and—"

"I get blunzed." Harry jumped up and down with excitement. "Let's get to work, Fletch. You're going to be in charge of the sequencing."

"Is it dangerous?"

"It's possible that all of central Jersey'll go up when those gluons hit the vortex coil. But of course—"

"We *know* it's going to work," I chortled. "Or you wouldn't have been able to make Godzilla happen yesterday."

Harry and I went over the procedure a few more times, and then he and Antie and I got to work putting everything together. Time passed.

Before I knew it, night had fallen. Someone was pounding at the front door.

"Who is it?" called Antie in her old woman's voice. "Who's there?"

"Sondra. Let me in, guys."

8

Magic Doors

"SONDRA, the point is to see it work. We know it works. That's why we built it. Fletcher, you talk to her. I'm going in the chamber now." Harry hovered near the heavy, copper-swathed door like a fat man entering a steam-bath.

"Good luck, Harry." I stepped forward and shook his hand. "The effects will last till midnight, right?"

"If I've got it calibrated correctly. We'll only use a hundred grams of the gluons. First I'll take care of the time travel and then I'll open up a door to another world."

"Why?" Sondra burst out. She'd been asking questions ever since we'd let her in, and she didn't seem to like the answers she'd been getting. I wished she would go away and let us destroy the universe in peace.

"Look," I said, "could you please just get out of the way?"

"So it's no girls allowed, huh? What if I call the cops?"

"Antie's a girl," said Harry. "Sort of. We're not doing anything illegal." He stood there, thinking, his hand on the fridge's door latch. "Sondra, I'm going to be master of space and time for two hours. Is there something you'd like me to do for you during that period of time? Wouldn't you like to have blond hair and a bod that won't quit?"

"He can make you look like Beva LeClaire," I suggested. Beva was the latest Hollywood sex symbol, the Marilyn Monroe of the 1990s. "Wouldn't you like that, Sondra?"

"I'd rather be able to fly."

"Done," said Harry. "Now shut up and watch." With a last nervous smile Harry stepped into the cubical blunzing chamber. A cloud of frost crystals billowed out, and then the refrigerator door slammed shut.

I slid aside a piece of the copper sheathing and peered in through the window we'd set into the door. Harry lay down on the hotshot table, waved his fist, and fitted on a breathing mask.

"Turn on the microwave, Antie."

"Check, Dr. F."

Harry slid back into a posture of noble ease. I covered up the little window and energized the copper sheathing.

"Antie, get the gluons."

Antie pincered up the heavy little magnetic bottle with one hand, grasping the lid with her other hand.

I opened the microwave cavity, which was a little black box like a miniature woodstove. A broad spectrum of radiation streamed out.

"Pour, Antie."

Antie came close and began pouring the gluons into the cavity. The gluons made up a sort of fluid, precious and sparkling as Christ's blood. The microwave energy field soaked the fluid right up.

As the gluons merged into the microwave field, the room filled with ethereal singing: faint, shifting notes almost too high to detect. A droplet of gluons slid down the lip of the magnetic bottle and burned the tip off one of Antie's fingers. I slammed the door of the little microwave cavity and breathed a sigh of relief. The first stage was completed.

"What was that stuff you poured in?" Sondra wanted to know. "It looked all irridescent, like fire and water mixed."

"Those were red gluons," I explained. "Usually they're hidden inside the protons and neutrons. I think they come in blue and yellow, too."

"Buried jewels," marveled Sondra. "Did they cost much?"

"You know it. We're saving half of them for the next time."

"Shall I energize the vortex coil, Dr. F.?"

"Check, Antie."

Antie threw the knife switch on the heavy power cable leading to the vortex coil, which was a hulking cone-shaped unit right next to the blunzing chamber. Ozone filled the air, and sparks crackled up and down the vortex coil's ridgy slopes. I saw the streetlights outside begin to dim.

"Initiate stage two."

I stepped back from the machinery as Antie devalved the subether wave guide, a heavily chromed duct leading from the microwave cavity to the vortex coil's rounded summit.

"Brace yourself, Sondra. This is—"

My words were drowned out by the chatter wild scream crash of tortured energy. The vortex coil was tearing into the gluons like a chain-saw hitting railroad spikes in water logs. The whole room went spastic shudder cow-eye thub scree thubby; my mind seized up. Flames, then a heavy sheet of sparks arcing from the coil to Antie's body. The faithful robot fused into dead smoking junk.

"Oh, poor Antie," wailed Sondra, starting forward.

"Stay back!" The screaming energy chatter slid up the scale to an insane mantric hum. The windows shattered. The fillings in my teeth were buzzing.

"Turn that knob!" I screamed to Sondra, pointing to the nozzle where the vacuum pump hooked into the blunzing chamber. "This is it!"

All I had to do now was to devalve the meter-long wave guide that led out of the vortex coil and in through the refrigerator wall to the needle at the hotshot table's head. But the wave guide was glowing hot. I cast about wildly, then spotted a broom. The handle would do the job. Just then there was a heavy thud: chamber at vacuum. Right on, Sondra. I forced myself forward and stabbed that final valve . . .

White light.

An angel was hovering over me, Beva LeClaire with big soft white wings. I was lying on a rustly mattress and the angel was floating over me.

"Are you all right, Joe?"

The voice: Sondra Tupperware! I sat up and looked around. This was Harry's workshop, same as before, and Antie was all well again, well and busy straightening up the mess we'd made. But Sondra—Sondra was hovering three feet off the floor, her wings gently aflutter. She wore a low-cut white evening dress; her face was a lovely cameo framed by ringlets of purest gold.

"I don't believe this," the angel was saying. "All my life I've hated women like this, and now I'm one."

"At least you can fly." I looked around for *my* goodies. And there they were, right under me, packs and packs of twenties and hundreds and five hundreds, a whole mattress of them! And next to my money-bed was a small wood box containing, no doubt, a simply reproducible device for turning dirt into food, just like I'd asked Harry for. Harry?

I hurried over to the blunzing chamber and dragged the big door open. "Harry!"

There he was, standing in the middle of the blunzing chamber. The hotshot table was gone. Harry was standing there with a swarm of little Harrys in the air around him. The little Harrys were all sizes, numberless as a column of spring gnats.

"Holy science, Harry! You really did it!"

"I've already done the trip back to Friday, and the lizard's trip, and I made your money and Nancy's cure for world hunger, and I moved the hotshot table out of the way." I noticed the table standing off to one side of the room. "And I fixed Antie—"

"What about me?" interrupted Sondra. "Flying milk van. I don't like it, Harry."

"Well, I do." Excitement parted his big lips. He stepped out of the blunzing chamber and looked around. "I like it this way." The swarm of little Harrys followed him out of the chamber.

"What are those things?" demanded Sondra. "Bugs?"

"They're little copies of me. There's infinitely many of them. It has to do with the renormalization problem and the existence of multiple solutions to the Schrödinger wave equation."

"They're little people?" said Sondra, stepping closer. She reached out a finger and one of the little Harrys landed on it. "How cute!"

"I can use them as scouts," said Harry. "That's what I'm going to do now." He herded the buzzing school of little Harrys back into the blunzing chamber, closed the door, and stood outside with his head pressed against the door. A minute passed, and another.

"There," Harry said finally. "It's done. Six worlds meet. Go on and look."

He stepped aside and I swung the blunzing chamber's door back open. What I saw inside was impossible. Somehow each of the cube's six faces were now an open door. I staggered and almost lost my footing.

Six doors to six places:
1. The room around us: Here and Now.
2. Globs and happy squiggles: The Microworld.
3. An endless meadowed mountain: Infinity.
4. Glowing robots on the moon: The Future.
5. Strange merging shapes: Hyperspace.

6. A room like ours, but upside down and backwards: Looking-Glass World.

From where I stood, Door No. 2 was to the left and Door No. 3 to the right. Door No. 4 was where the blunzing chamber's floor had been, and Door No. 5 was on the chamber's ceiling. Straight across the chamber was Door No. 6. Door No. 1, of course, was the original door, the door I stood outside.

The swarm of tiny Harrys buzzed fretfully, darting in and out of the six magic doors.

"Let's go," said the big Harry at my side. "Come on, Fletch, I want to jump across to that world on the other side."

"Forget it, man. I want to take my money back to Nancy before—"

"Oh, you've got your five million bucks and that's it, huh? Only so far and no further, right? What are you going to buy, Fletcher? What's going to be as good as this?"

I looked to Sondra for support. She was staring into a mirror, running her fingers over the curves of her new face.

I tried again. "Harry, those doors look really exciting. Hyperspace, size change, parallel worlds—it looks really neat. But I'm not going to risk everything just for some crazy science fiction thrills."

"I can still make your money disappear, Fletcher. I can put you back inside an endless regress like before."

"You don't want to do that, Harry. I'm your friend, remember? Just go ahead and enjoy yourself. Sondra and I'll wait out here."

Sondra fluttered over to stand next to us. Lord, she was gorgeous.

"Make my wings disappear," she requested. "I don't want to be a freak. Surely you can give me flight without wings."

"Damn!" yelled Harry, suddenly furious. "Here I'm supposed to be the master of space and time and you two are just—" He clenched his eyes shut like an angry baby.

There was a faint whisking sound, and Sondra's wings were gone. My money and my little box—I noticed sadly—were gone as well.

"Gee, Harry, you didn't have to—"

"Your money's safe at home, Fletcher. Right under little Nancy's homebody bed. And she's opening her dirt-to-food converter right now." A sly smile twisted his mouth. "You satisfied?"

"Yeah, I guess."

"Now, please, you two, let's go across the chamber and into the looking-glass world. I'm scared to go alone."

I looked into Sondra's clear hazel eyes. I'd never been this close to such a beautiful woman before. "I'll go if Sondra will."

"Okay, Sondra?"

"Oh, all right. I'll help fly Fletcher across. We wouldn't want him to fall down onto the moon with those robots. But what's the looking-glass world supposed to be, Harry?"

"It's where I want to go. I don't know quite what's there ... I just know I reached out and found it."

"Found it?"

"Each reality is a point in superspace," said Harry

slowly. "I understand everything so much better now! Superspace has infinitely many dimensions, one dimension for each question you might ask about the world. Each universe represents a certain set of answers, a certain location in superspace. I reached out and found the one I wanted, the looking-glass world."

"What about those four other worlds?"

"They're—they're other things I've thought about. I understand them pretty well already. Some of my little echomen have already looked them over. But come on now, let's go to the looking-glass world! And Antie, you make sure that no one disturbs the machinery while we're gone."

"Check, Harry."

Sondra could still fly, even without those hokey wings, and Harry of course had the power of flight as well. Each grabbed me under an arm, and we flew the two meters across the blunzing chamber.

The view from the chamber's center was just incredible. There was no gravity in there, and the conflicting vistas through the different doors destroyed all sense of up and down. Hypercubes, amoebas, infinite cliffs, space robots—all mixed in with glimpses of Harry's shop. The room we were headed for was upside down and mirror-reversed relative to the room we'd started in.

I wondered what it was going to be like over there.

9
Looking-Glass World

As we passed into the looking-glass world, its gravity took over and pulled me up to its floor. I tucked my head under and landed on my shoulders. Regaining my feet, I looked back through the magic door at the world we'd left. Antie was there, standing by the door watching us. It was hard not to feel that it was the robot, and not us, who was upside down.

The little images of Harry flew out after us and nested themselves together like they'd done in my car. Each of them got in the coat pocket of the next larger one. It only took a few seconds. Then the biggest echoman of all darted into the real Harry's pocket.

"Let's just close the door," suggested Harry. "So nothing sneaks back through to our world."

"Okay."

I helped him swing the heavy zinc-covered door shut. Although it was late evening in the world we'd left, it looked like midmorning here. Sunlight was streaming in the windows, lighting up the mirror-reversed shop.

"Well!" said Sondra. "Now what, guys?"

"Let's go to a restaurant," I suggested. "Get a beer and listen to what people are talking about. I hope time doesn't run backwards here."

"Naw," said Harry. "Look." He picked up a book and dropped it. It fell to the floor. "If our time didn't match this world's, we would have seen the book fly up into my hand."

"Yeah," I agreed, leaning over the book. "But look, all the writing's backwards."

"Well, that's no big deal. Everything's just space-reversed. Once we get outside, we'll probably find lots of other differences as well. Like Carroll's Alice did. Let's go, we've got less than two hours!"

We found our way out of Harry's mirror-reversed shop and hit the street. The streets were *clean,* that was what struck me first. The whole city was buffed to an unwholesome sheen. Spotless late-model autos hurried past in orderly queues, while spiffed-up pedestrians marched up and down like wooden soldiers. Slovenly Harry couldn't have looked more out of place. At least the tiny Harrys were stashed out of sight. This town looked nothing like New Brunswick: besides being clean, it felt vaguely Arabian. I didn't like the fact that nobody smiled.

"Excuse me," I said, stepping in front of a woman in a stiff-collared blouse. She had gray hair and a dowager's hump. "Is there a restaurant near here? That sells beer?"

Her thin lips straightened. "I'm going to report you for that, you scum."

"Beer's illegal?" I hazarded, hoping to keep the conversational ball rolling.

"Let me pass!"

"Wait," protested Sondra. "We just got here from another world and—"

"Demons!" screamed the woman in the stiff-collared blouse. Two men in three-piece suits hurried to her aid.

"Let's fly," I suggested.

Harry and Sondra grabbed me by the upper arms again, and we shot up into the air. There was a cop on the sidewalk across the street, shouting and pointing a laser rifle.

We whisked off across the building tops and landed in a supermarket parking lot. Fortunately no one saw us land.

"Do you realize what this world is?" I asked Harry.

"Uh . . ."

"It's the exact opposite of everything you like. Clean streets, uptight women, no beer. Everything's backwards, you idiot." I could hear sirens a few blocks off.

"The police are coming," wailed Sondra. "Do something, Harry!"

"I'm not always good in a crisis," he whined. "Ask Fletcher what to do."

"Let's go in that store," I suggested. "After things cool down, we can get back to the magic door."

"Okay."

Instead of glass doors, the supermarket had air curtains. These were sheets of cool air blown down from a grate overhead to be sucked into a grate in the threshold. We breezed into the store and looked around. Oh, man.

No-cal soft drinks, weight-watcher TV dinners, and diet junk food, all heavily vitaminized. This provender was at a double remove from reality: it was artificially made food that had been further treated in an attempt to make it healthy. There was nothing real in sight: no meat, no veggies, no booze.

I began to lose my temper. "What would you like, Harry? You can bet it's not here. God, you're stupid. Who else would go to a world the exact opposite of what he wants? Just look at this crap!" I kicked at a bin of one-calorie cupcakes.

"Watch your language, fella!" A round-shouldered man who must have been the manager poked his head around some shelves to glare at us. His face was coarse and humorless. When he spotted Sondra his cheeks grew red. "And get that slut out of here! She's practically naked!"

I sprang to Sondra's defense. Sure she had big breasts and a low-cut dress, but that didn't make her any less a friend. Far from it. I stepped threateningly toward the manager. "You're the one who'd better watch his language, jerk. Slug him, Harry!"

No one was watching, so Harry went ahead and punched the man in the stomach. What with Harry's superpowers, the punch doubled the manager right up. Eager to do my part for Sondra, I reached out and slammed my fist down on the hump between the man's shoulder blades.

To my surprise the hump was soft. It burst with a muffled *plotz*, and fluid began seeping through the manager's coat. The poor man's body shivered a few times and then he was dead.

"Oh, my God," I said in horror. "I—I didn't mean to kill him. I never thought that—"

"I'll move it out of here before someone sees it," Harry said tensely. "I can do teleportation. Just . . ."

Harry knitted his brows, and then the body was gone. I felt better almost immediately. This world wasn't really real, was it?

"That was bad," said Sondra. "Let's leave."

"We might as well get a couple of six packs of soda," I suggested. "Once we're outside, Harry can turn them into beer. We'll steal a car and go cruising."

"Sound thinking, Fletch. The old water-to-wine routine."

"That was nice of you two to stick up for me," mused Sondra. "Being beautiful isn't always pleasant. Do you think our money's good here?"

"We'll see. Be ready for trouble."

We took our place in the checkout line. A few people stared at Sondra with mingled lust and hatred, but for the moment everything was cool. I watched the checker, trying to anticipate any problems.

The checker was a pleasant-faced blond woman with *Burnita* on her name tag. She wore a gold chain with a pendant—a little silver chair. She scanned each product with a little light pencil. Everything had a patch of thick and thin lines, a Universal Product Code, just like back home. A cord fed the UPC information into a small console at Burnita's side. But instead of presenting each customer with a bill, she ran the light pencil across the client's forehead. Apparently there was some kind of invisible Universal Consumer Code tattooed on each of these people's brows. An efficient system, to be sure: a central computer could deduct your purchases from your credit holdings on a real-time basis. But, I wondered, what would happen if you let yourself become badly overdrawn?

Just then I found out. The customer in front of us was a ratlike little man with a tube of cheese food and three bottles of cough medicine. Clearly an unsavory individual, and just the type to let his credit holdings slip deep into the red.

Burnita seemed to feel the same way, and addressed him by name. "Now, Abie, are you sure you've got the credit for all this?"

Abie snarled something incoherent and pushed his selections toward the checker. She shrugged, and scanned first the product codes and then the invisible code on Abie's forehead. Nothing happened, and I breathed a sigh of relief. We were next. I reached in my pocket, feeling for some bills. Surely you didn't *have* to use credit. I hoped not, because all our foreheads were blank, which might . . .

FFZZZAAAAAATT!

A great sheet of electricity filled the supermarket entrance. Those two air-curtain grates were electrodes, powerful energy sources programmed to crisp anyone who ran up too high a tab. Abie's ashes spun raggedly. The floor grate sucked them out of sight.

"Oh, my," Burnita sighed. "That's the second one this week. It's hard for them, you know, since there's no other way to get food. You folks just want these sodas?" I suddenly realized that the little silver chair hanging from Burnita's neck was an electric chair.

"Uh, wait." I drew out some money. "Can we pay cash?"

The checker's pleasant face grew tense and puzzled. "Is this some kind of joke? Come on, folks, which of you should I bill?" She raised the light pen toward my forehead. God only knew what would happen if they found out we were uncoded.

"Harry! Get us out of here!"

A moment of disorientation and then we were back outside in the parking lot. A harsh alarm bell was ringing.

"As long as you can do teleportation, Harry, why not just take us back to the blunzing chamber?"

"Aw, that wouldn't be any fun. I want to keep the super-stuff to a minimum. And what's the big rush to leave? We just got here!"

"Let's steal a car like Joe said," urged Sondra. "I've always wanted to be a big blond in a stolen getaway car."

"What are we getting away with?" I asked sourly.

"The soda!" Prettily she raised the two six-packs up like earrings. She looked like Marilyn in *The Misfits*.

"It's beer now," said Harry. "Let's take that Cad."

We piled into a big white Cadillac with black leather upholstery. Sondra got in front with Harry, and I got in back with the beer. It was nice and roomy in there, almost as big as my bedroom back in Princeton. I wondered if Nancy was worried about me yet.

Harry psych-started the car and peeled out.

"There must be a bad part of town," he muttered, slewing into the traffic. "That's where we should go. Someone there'll tell us what's really going on here. I think we should try and overthrow the government." Harry dodged some cars and gave a whoop of laughter. We were still accelerating.

"This is neat," Sondra giggled. "Give me a beer, Joe."

"You two are getting overconfident," I warned. "If some cop shoots us from behind, then Harry's superpowers aren't going to be worth a damn." Grudgingly I opened three beers. Ah.

Harry flipped on the radio. It was an evangelist, of course, this being a world of bad choices.

". . . hatred," said the radio. "Yes, *hatred*, my fellow Herberites. Gary came to preach hatred. I know this may sound strange to some of you out there in the radio audience, but it's *not* a matter of conjecture. God hates the unbeliever, just as the unbeliever hates Gary Herber. Yes, friends, it's true. Just look at the facts! On the one hand, we have Seth and Gary Herber bringing the clean wholesomeness of God's Laws. On the other, we have the unbelievers, with their trumped-up charges and their public electrocution. Seth Herber died, yes, he died for mankind. But thanks to the blessed Scionization, Gary Herber lives with thousands of us, friends, and he's ready to—"

A laser blast shattered our rear window. Cops behind us, gaining fast. I threw myself down on the seat. "Teleportation time, Harry. Can you handle the whole car?"

"No problem."

Disorientation again, and then we were coasting

down a street of abandoned Moorish-style white stucco buildings with parapets around their flat roofs. Hard, midday sun overhead. The sirens were far away. Harry pulled up onto the curb and we got out. Shadows moved behind the buildings' broken windows.

"This looks like the right place," said Sondra, radiant in her white evening dress. She finished her beer and threw the can in the street. "I wonder who that Gary person is."

A rock flew down from one of the rooftop terraces and crashed through our car's windshield.

"I wish we had some guns," I said.

"Look in the trunk," offered Harry.

The trunk was unlatched, of course, and there were three bright plastic pistols, real sf-looking, with fins and knobs and dials all over them.

"This is a matter disintegrator," said Harry, handing me the purple one. "That dial up there makes the beam fan out."

"Thanks."

"Sondra, you take the pink one. It's a demotivator. Makes things stop moving."

"Oooooooo," she squealed, and snatched her toy. Sondra was really starting to camp it up. She'd waited a long time to be beautiful.

"And I'll keep this green one."

"What does the green one *do*, Harry?"

"It makes time go backwards."

"Oooooooooo!" A toss of her pretty blond hair. Sondra and Harry were having fun. I wished I could relax and enjoy this, too.

Three more rocks came flying down, one at each of us. We raised our pistols and fired.

My rock shattered and was gone. Sondra's rock stopped falling and hung in midair. Harry's rock reversed its motion and flew back up to the rooftop it had come from. There was a faint scream.

"Let's fly up and meet our friend," I suggested.

10
God's Laws

On the roof was a gaunt man wearing a fedora. The rock Harry had sent back was lying at the man's feet. Sondra froze him with the demotivator and we frisked him. He seemed clean: no weapons, no machinery.

"Check in his hat," Harry suggested.

Sure enough, the hat's sweatband hid a ring of circuit cards and microprobes. Apparently the hat had been feeding signals in and out of the gaunt man's brain—probably for pleasure. The guy had the wasted air of a stim-addict.

"Okay, Sondra," said Harry, "turn off your ray." Harry was taking chances, too many chances. I decided to break things up.

"Wait a second, Sondra. Just hold it right there. Before this goes any further, I think the three of us had better have a talk. What time is it?"

"It's ten-thirty," said Harry, glancing at his watch. "Okay, now, Sondra—"

"Will you just let me talk? It's ten-thirty. Does that mean we have one and a half hours left?"

"Yeah, that's right. Thursday noon here matches Sunday midnight in New Brunswick. Everything backward, simple as pie."

"What?"

"From *Thursday noon* to *Sunday midnight* it's three and a half days either way, so—"

"Will I still be able to fly after twelve?" interrupted Sondra. "And will I still look like this?" I turned away from Harry to watch her talk. The movement of her red lips. Her breathy voice. Her platinum hair. "Because I'm getting used to it, and I think I could do a lot of good for Scientific Mysticism. We have to be sure to go back through that magic door before twelve, Harry darling." She batted her eyes at him.

"Yeah," said Harry, slipping his arm around her waist. "The changes will stay, but the magic doors will stop working. Keeping them open is like a constant series of wishes. We could get stuck in this looking-glass world if we're not careful. But don't worry, I'll teleport us all back to the door in plenty of time."

"How about now?" I demanded. "While we're still alive and everything."

"You are so uptight, Fletcher. Don't you like it here? I'm having fun."

Something dawned on me then. "This really is the perfect world for you, isn't it, Harry? Of all the possible worlds in superspace, this is the one you'd pick even if you knew what you were doing."

"That's right," said Harry, grinning broadly. The bright sun made his face look like a black-and-white photograph. The roof was tiled, with a waist-high parapet. There was a staircase set down into the roof's center. "What's the good of having superpowers if you don't have a world to save?" Harry went on. "Sometime during the next hour and a half we're going to get to that God-pig Gary Herber and assassinate him. The people here will thank us forever. I've never seen a religion that wasn't basically evil."

"Gary Herber?"

"Gary Herber's the one that preacher was talking about on the car radio. He's some kind of big prophet here. I figure everything bad here is Herber's doing."

Gary Herber. I turned the name over in my mind. Of course. It was all beginning to make sense. "I guess you realize who Gary Herber really *is*, don't you, Harry?"

"Harry Gerber!" squealed Sondra. "Gary Herber!"

Harry looked a little unsettled. He *hadn't* realized. "Uh . . ."

"It's your mirror self," said Sondra. "Your other nature. You've objectified the repressed side of your personality so as to do battle with it. How Jungian!"

Harry looked more and more uneasy. "Damn. I hope this Herber guy doesn't look too much like me."

It made me feel better to see Harry look so worried. "You know the old line, Harry. *Inside every fat man there's a thin man fighting to get out.*

Gary Herber's probably real thin. And clean." My mouth framed a hard grin.

"Our Harry's not dirty," squealed Sondra, slipping back into her blond bombshell routine. "*Are* you, honey?" She gave a shrill giggle and pinched Harry's cheek.

"You can turn off your ray now, Sondra."

Sondra lowered her pretty pink pistol, and the gaunt man started talking. "I need my hat." His thin-lipped mouth formed a faint, gentlemanly smile. "The sun's mighty bright up here."

I held the hat out of reach. "Just wait a minute. What's all the circuitry in the sweatband for? And why were you throwing rocks at us?"

"I've got to have my hat, mister." His voice was papery and far away. Still I hesitated, and his faint smile twitched into an agonized rictus. His whole body began to shake, though his flat, burnt eyes stayed calm. "I'm not making it too good."

"He's a wirehead," said Harry. "His hat's a stim-unit. Let him have it back."

I handed the gaunt man his fedora. With precise, twitching gestures, he got it snugged down on his bony skull. His eyelids dropped and the shaking stopped.

"Seeing with my mouth," he murmured. "Should take off more often. Running out of lobes." He got his eyes back open and fixed me with a hard stare. "You're coming on real tiresome."

"Can you help us?" asked Harry. "We're from another world and we think we want to kill Gary Herber."

The stranger chuckled slowly. "Kicks, man, kicks. But Herber's awful big. Used to be he was just a yahoo and a brain full of truth. But ever since they electrocuted him . . ." The man in the hat chuckled again, and went off on a tangent. "I had a booth selling pieces of the electric chair. 'Relics of the Scionization,' you dig, all splinters smeared with rancid ghee." He paused to give me a look of unwholesome flirtation. "I threw the rocks because you look so rave."

I cleared my throat. What kind of guide had Harry dreamed up for us? "I'm Joe Fletcher. And that's Sondra and Harry."

"Joe." He touched my face with his cool fingers. "It's a rare pleasure to meet an intelligent man. I'm Tad Beat."

"How about a drink?" asked Harry. "Do you have any whiskey?"

"I have enough to get you boys country drunk. Let's make my pad."

We followed Tad downstairs. His apartment took up one very large room on the building's top floor. His floor and walls were covered with Oriental carpets. A narrow bed, some boxes of food, and a desk with papers and a typewriter completed the furnishings.

"Stap my vitals," muttered Tad, rummaging under his bed. "Just what the old doctor ordered. Keeps the slugs off, too." He took out a clear glass bottle of oily liquid.

Harry drank from it, wiped his mouth, then passed the bottle to Sondra. She shook her head and gave the bottle to me. It was moonshine, sharp and with a bitter undertaste. I spit out half the mouthful I'd taken and gave the bottle back to Tad. I didn't trust wireheads.

"Tell us more about Herber," I requested. "Did he start a religion, or what? You say they electrocuted him?"

"You're really elsewhere," said Tad. "Mr. Nobody from Nowhere. Scope this, age levels five through thirteen."

He handed me a color comic book, the kind of thing that a child might bring home from Bible school. On the cover was a soft giant brain with a halo. That was Gary? Crowded all around the brain were laughing children with humps on their backs. It occurred to me that I'd seen a lot of round-shouldered people on the streets here. Why would being saved make you into a hunchback? Beginning to sense my answer, I sat down and read the comic book frame by frame. The writing was mirror-reversed, but I got used to that soon enough.

1. *Gary's parents were scientists.* Two clean-cut people in white smocks. She holds a test tube, he holds a Geiger counter.

2. *Their world was full of trouble.* Weapons, broken liquor bottles, bloody faces, a background of psychedelic music symbols.

3. *And God had been forgotten.* A drunk sleeping on the steps of a looted temple.

4. *God spoke to Gary's parents.* They stand in a roomful of machines, staring up into streaming light.

5. *And told them what to do.* She leans over a microscope, while he handles some radioactive material with tongs. Her belly is swollen.

6. *Gary Herber was born on June 25.* The parents lean over a radiant cradle. The cradle contains a naked brain with a spinal cord.

7. *Gary's brother, Seth, was scared.* The brain floats

in a tank of nutrient. A dirty, unattractive boy peers at it from around a doorjamb.

8. *God told Seth to share.* Seth kneeling next to the brain's tank, his face blank with religious ecstasy.

9. *Seth and Gary grew together.* Gary is riding the nape of Seth's neck. Seth is clean and happy-looking, writing answers on a blackboard.

10. *They began to teach God's Laws.* Lean and charismatic, Seth is standing on a soapbox preaching to a crowd. The naked brain is hidden beneath Seth's coat.

11. *These are God's Laws.* A stone tablet with three laws chiseled in:

God's Laws
I: Follow Gary
II: Be Clean
III: Teach God's Laws

Tad thrust the bottle at me again. Reluctantly I looked up from the comic. The bottle was almost empty and Harry was drunk. He was sitting on Tad's bed with his arm around Sondra. They were kissing.

"No thanks, Tad." I turned my attention back to the comic. "Is this all true?"

"They omit to mention where Gary wig and drink all a woman's spinal fluid. She croaked and the Herbers got the chair."

I read on.

12. *Gary's disciples shared him.* Smiling Seth is setting Gary down on an attractive woman's naked

back. Many cheering faces in the background.

13. *But there were enemies.* Three swarthy, low-browed men sitting at a table with money and whiskey. One shows a legal document to his gloating comrades.

14. *Seth and Gary were arrested.* Faceless police officers in riot helmets drag humpbacked Seth away from weeping women and children.

15. *The public electrocution.* Seth is strapped into an electric chair. A special wire leads to Gary, naked on Seth's back. A crowd is watching.

16. *The Blessed Scionization.* Seth is dead and smoking. But Gary is much bigger than before. He bulges out like a cauliflower, and pieces of him are splitting off.

17. *Soon Gary was everywhere.* An army of men, women, and children, each with a naked brain riding on his or her back. They are constructing a palace.

18. *Don't you want to share?* The tablet of God's Laws, the electric chair, and a cheerful brain float together in a space of light.

19. *Come to the Palace this Thursday!* Two happy children, a boy and a girl, walk up the marble steps of a splendid white building.

I closed the comic and looked up. Tad and Sondra were arguing. Harry was really out of it, and Tad had just given him another bottle.

"Why do you give him so much to drink?" Sondra demanded.

"It's like the sight of someone about to flip excites me," Tad said, reaching up to fondle his hatband. "I like to crack them open and feed on the wonderful soft stuff that ooze out."

Sondra looked at Tad with real dislike. "You're awful! A wirehead, a drunk, a gay—"

Tad leered at her, forming his face into a caricature of heterosexual lust. "What are these strange feelings that come over me when I look at those tits sticking out so cute? No, no!" He held his hand as if to shield his face, then sidled over to drape his arms across my shoulders. "You and me could really exist, Joe."

Harry was taking this all in with drunken relish.

"We don't have very much time," I said, fending off Tad's advances. He was a real old-time degenerate.

Harry chugged from the new bottle and tossed it back to Tad. I didn't see how they could stomach the stuff. I felt sick from the one taste of it I'd had.

"Just tell us where to find Gary Herber," said Sondra. "And we'll be on our way."

"It's not going to be as easy as we thought," I told her. "Herber is all over the place. He's a sort of parasite that grows on people's backs. But what was that about a palace, Tad?"

"Gary's palace," said Tad, smiling loosely. "Ten blocks east of here. The palace is for the boss slug. The king-size Herber that grows the buds. Granpaw brain. We'll hold him still with that pink gun and work out. Do it hard TV so's the citizens down home can share the harvest plenty." Tad seemed almost as drunk as Harry.

Sondra and I exchanged looks of concern. It was well past eleven.

"We really have to get moving," I repeated.

"Don't you want to try on my hat, Joe? It has a

left-brain/right-brain feedback loop. Feel real wiggy."

"No!" cried Sondra. "Let's go before it's too late!"

We clattered down the stone stairs to the street, Harry leaning heavily on Tad and me. Sondra flew down ahead of us.

"Do you want me to drive, Harry?"

"Naw, naw, I'm shuperman. I'll shober up when I hafta. You wanna gun, Tad? Look in the glove compartment."

Tad found himself a heavy .45 automatic. We all got in the Cad. Both of the windshields were broken—the police laser had broken the back, and Tad's rock had broken the front. Harry gunned the engine up to a chattering scream, and peeled out into a teleportation jump.

11

cushion

WE were speeding down a broad boulevard, a tropical *allée* with rows of royal palms: tremendous palm trees each with ten meters of bare trunk topped by a luxuriant green frizz-bop of swordy leaves. The pavement was smooth marble. There was quite a bit of traffic: official vehicles, merchants' vans, tour buses, commuters. But there was no real congestion—everyone drove according to the book. The cars moved like cautious ants, and the pedestrians marched back and forth like windup toys.

Far ahead of us, tiny in the distance, was a cordon of white-uniformed palace guards. Beyond the guards lay bright ornamental gardens leading to the palace itself, a vast, minaretted structure something like the Taj Mahal.

I was in the back seat with Tad Beat. He twitched

his head this way and that, keeping a restless eye on things. Harry, in front, lolled drunkenly in his seat, pawing at Sondra's exposed thighs and protesting in slurred tones each time she slapped his hand away. Our Cadillac lurched through the traffic, narrowly missing several collisions.

"He's juiced," Tad said to me, jerking his head toward Harry's slumping shoulders. Tad kept one hand on his hat, holding it tight against the slipstream of air that whistled through the car's two broken windshields. "That's the cool way to be around the palace. The slugs can't handle juice. You, Joe, you're nowhere. You'll end up dead or a Herberite, I'll tell you now."

Tad's words sent a chill through my veins. With Harry so drunk, what chance did we stand against those guards? If I died here, would I really be dead? This was really just a kind of dream, wasn't it? Yet what if you have a dream so bad that you die of a heart attack during the dream? Perhaps *every time* someone dies in his sleep of a heart attack, the attack is in fact coupled with a dream of overwhelming power in which the person experiences death in great detail. Who can tell?

The palace guards were only some fifty meters ahead of us now. They could see there was something fishy about us. As we drew closer, they raised their weapons and aimed.

"All right," said Harry in his normal voice. He'd willed himself sober, just like that. He sat up straight and stepped on the gas. "Beam them, Fletch. You can shoot over my shoulder."

I dialed my disintegrator ray to maximum fan and blasted away. I was already a murderer from smashing that supermarket manager's spine-rider. Kill one, kill twenty. Most of the palace guards turned to dust. The survivors took to their heels. I retched up a mouthful of stomach acid. Killing wasn't something I could learn to enjoy.

Harry kept the hammer down, and we smashed through a set of ironwork gates. There were marble stairs up ahead. We took them like we had square wheels. The lovely gardens were all around us, fountains and geometric beds of flowers. Some pretty women with bare backs were lounging on the lawns.

A hot beam of red laser light speared down from one of the palace's slim watchtowers. The beam burned a hole in our Cadillac's hood, and then the engine died.

"I'll handle that," said Harry. He aimed his time-reversing ray gun at the distant laser cannon. Our engine started back up, the hole in the hood sealed over, and the laser energy returned to its source. Smoke poured out of that slim minaret—smoke and screams.

Our car stumbled up a last marble staircase and coughed to a stop. The four of us jumped out, guns at the ready. We were standing under a huge, pillared portico. Before us was the palace entrance, a Moorish arch with massive bronze doors. The doors were open and unguarded.

I felt weak and sick, but Harry's drunkenness was miraculously gone. Master of space and time.

Sondra was in high gear. "What's your anti-self going to look like, Harry? Tad and Joe say it's a giant slug. Let's be sure to steal some jewels after we kill it. I guess you know it's already eleven twenty-five? We better hurry. I can't wait for my friend Donna to see my new look. Maybe I'll go on TV. Do you think Dr. Bitter will approve?"

"That big Gary Herber's in the central courtyard," said Tad. "Let's hang real tight."

He went in first, then Harry and Sondra, then me.

Something dropped onto the nape of my neck just as I walked through the door.

Oh, no! The soft moist Herber-slug slid down between my shoulder blades and plugged itself into my nervous system. I felt a wild tingling.

"duck into the next doorway," said a little voice in my head. The voice of the parasitic glob that had just taken over my will. I struggled to yell to the others, but instead I whipped in through the first doorway we passed.

"Fletch?" called Harry from the hall. "Where'd he go, Sondra? HEY, FLETCHER!"

I was running as fast as my legs would carry me. Through a cloakroom, out into a courtyard, through a door, and into a bedroom. There was a woman, a naked odalisque on a big mound of cushions. She had jet-black hair and lily-white skin. Almond eyes, a long straight nose, large nipples, heavy-duty thighs. I burrowed under her cushions like a rat taking cover. It felt nice down there: the silky cushions, the woman's odor and weight. I tried to wriggle into a position where I'd be able to . . .

"be still," said the voice in my head.

I stopped moving and thought a message back: *"who are you?"*

"i'm a scion of gary herber. thank you for your body."

"i wasn't really done with it yet." For some reason I was kind of enjoying this. The parasite kept a pleasant tingle going all through my nerves. *"you'll have to release me, i'm from another world."*

"i know. we want to go there."

"no! you can't! it's—"

"shhh!"

Footsteps sounded in the courtyard outside. Fat Harry, weird Tad, and sexy Sondra. They'd never find me here. I should have been screaming for help, but instead I felt like giggling. The slug had really taken me over.

"Uh, excuse me, miss, have you seen my friend?" Harry's voice.

The odalisque shifted about, but she didn't answer.

"She won't pick up on you," said Tad. "Herber's dollies don't talk to strangers."

"What would a giant brain want with slave girls?" asked Sondra.

"What Gary wants with women? He milks them, like. GABA fluid from their spines. You dig that plastic coupling down on her back?"

"Oooooo! Awful! Well, read her mind, Harry. You can do telepathy, can't you?"

"Stap my vitals!" exclaimed Tad. "Telepathy!"

"Yeah, I can do it," rumbled Harry, "but that would be too—"

"Harry, in less than half an hour, our magic door out of this place is going to disappear. And now something's happened to Joe. Use your goddamn telepathy or I'll—"

"Oh, all right."

". . . *cushion* . . ." was all that me and my rider were thinking. A masquerade. We held our joint consciousness in the mind-set of a ". . . *cushion* . . ."

The odalisque must have some kind of block up too. After a minute Harry stopped scanning. I could feel the difference. "I don't find him anywhere, Sondra. But I think he's hiding somewhere nearby."

"Why would he hide?"

"Oh, Fletcher's weird. He's weirder than you realize, Sondra. People always say that *I'm* crazy, but Fletcher is much worse. He's *sneaky* about being crazy. The guy needs help, I mean it."

". . . *cushion* . . ."

"Well, what are we going to do?"

"Let's go ahead and kill that giant brain," urged Tad. "You've got to do that for us before you leave."

"But what about Joe," protested Sondra. "We can't just forget about him."

". . . *cushion* . . ."

"If he gets stuck here, it's his own damn fault. He's hiding from me, I tell you. He's got a telepathy block up, and this woman has one too. I can't read anyone's mind but yours and Tad's, Sondra."

"Ooooooo! What are we thinking, Harry?"

"You don't want to know. Tad, which way is it to the central courtyard? I'll teleport the three of us there. Maybe Gary Herber can tell us where Fletcher is."

"That's cool," said Tad. "Joe's probably wearing a brain on his back right now. The courtyard is— that way, about one hundred meters."

"Okay."

The voices disappeared. I crawled out from under the cushions and sat up. The big odalisque licked her lips. She had a large tongue and a cruel mouth. I sighed and laid my head down on her shoulder. She ran one hand over my face, and with her other hand she drew a few drops of spinal fluid out of the tap at the bottom of her back. Gently she rubbed the fluid into my spine-rider. I shuddered with pleasure. This was really living.

"where is the door to your world?" The slug's sudden question caught me by surprise.

"i can't tell you that."

"you must."

A silent struggle ensued. The spine-rider probed at my thoughts, trying to winkle out the precious secret. I sought to hide the secret in jingles, in emotions, in hebephrenic repetitions of random fact. But the parasite was too strong for me. In less than a minute I was beaten. The image of the street where we'd arrived formed in my mind. The spine-rider goaded me to my feet.

"Please call a taxi," I heard myself telling the handsome dark-haired woman. "And make sure the driver has a Herber scion."

She picked up a telephone and began dialing.

"And take this disintegrator ray," my voice added. "It may prove useful in the fight against those three intruders."

The woman took my gun and spoke softly into the phone.

"that gun isn't going to help against Harry," I thought to the bad brain on my back. *"he's master of space*

and time. if he gets mad he'll wipe out big Gary and every single one of you scions."

"all the more reason to send one of us over to your world. now, run!"

12

Midnight Rambler

I ran back out the palace the way I'd come in Some humpbacked guards were out on the portico, but since I too had a spine-rider, they let me pass. I ran all the way down to the street. I was exhausted and out of breath, but my scion wouldn't let me stop.

Just as I got to the curb, a taxi pulled up. I jumped in the front, and we took off. The driver was a tall, muscle-faced man with round shoulders. Instead of addressing him directly, I pulled up our shirts and let our Gary-brains touch. Once the driver got the picture, he really stepped on the gas.

Looking out the window I tried to tell which of the pedestrians wore a scion on his or her back. Only about one in ten. Yet the others were so beaten down by Herber's rule that they might just as well have had one of the parasites plugged into their nervous systems. No one smiled; there was no sense of play. This was a city of statistics, of interchangeable bodies carrying out Gary Herber's tasks. I felt like a cockroach in an anthill.

Yet all the while the tingling in my nerves continued to fill me with a sort of secret pleasure. I may have looked like a zombie, but on some level I was having fun. It was perhaps a little like being a wirehead. I watched the scenery whip past and tried not to think about what came next.

The taxi pulled up to the spot where this whole adventure had started. There was the mirror image of Harry's shop. The driver and I hurried inside. The copy of the blunzing chamber was still there: a big metal box, two meters on a side.

"send him through and then destroy it!" said the voice in my head.

Send him through? I took a good look at the driver. He was a strong, mean-looking character with short black hair. Send him through and let the Herber-scions invade Earth? *"no,"* I protested, *"please not that."*

A lash of pain swept up my spine and into my skull. I fought it as long as I could and lost again. Numbly I watched myself open the blunzing chamber's door. Over on the other side I could see upside-down Antie, still waiting for her master.

The Gary-brained driver took a running jump and leaped through the magic door. He flipped, landed smoothly on the other side, and took off at a run. Tears welled out of my eyes and streamed down my cheeks. My arms swung the door shut.

"now let's smash it," said the voice in my head. *"i want my brother brain to be safe from harry."*

My body hurried across the room to pick up a sledgehammer I'd noticed before. My arms put all their strength into the first blow, and the hammer smashed a hole in one of the chamber's sides.

It was the side that led into the Microworld. A pseudopod lashed out from the hole I'd made and ingested the head of my hammer. When I managed to pull it free, my sledgehammer was just an axe handle with an acid-charred end. The giant Microworld amoeba pushed another pseudopod out of the hole and felt around. My spine-rider and I backed off in some confusion.

Just then there was a *pop* and a rush of air. It was Harry and Sondra. I raised my axe handle and charged at Harry. My Herber-slug wanted me to smash Harry's skull in. But Harry and Sondra had been expecting trouble. Sondra raised her pink demotivator ray and froze me in mid-lunge.

"It's Fletcher!" exclaimed Harry. "My worst enemy? Here we've been over at the palace killing that giant brain and here's my so-called pal Fletcher trying to tear down our magic door!"

Harry walked around behind me, careful to stay out of Sondra's beam. I felt my shirt slide up.

"Wearing a brain, sure enough," Harry rumbled. "Well, I'll just—"

A wave of murderous agony began to build inside my skull. That bad brain was going to kill me with it. I prayed a last prayer and prepared to merge into the One. But then—*phht*—the pain and the spine-rider were all gone. Harry had simply willed it out of existence.

"Turn off the ray, Sondra. He's clean."

Slowly I arched my back. My body was my own again.

"Oh, God, Harry, it wasn't my fault. That—*thing* was part of Gary Herber. There's thousands of them all over the city."

"It's eleven fifty-six," Sondra called tautly.

"It's okay, Fletch, I know it's not your fault. Too bad you had to give that Arab-looking woman your disintegrator ray, though. She killed poor Tad, and almost got Sondra and me, too."

"But you took care of the big brain?"

"Yeah. And now I'm going to get all the little ones." Harry reached into his coat pocket and took out the thumb-sized "echo" of himself that the blunzing chamber had produced. He snapped the little fellow in the air like a handkerchief, and an endless swarm of smaller Harrys appeared as well.

"Okay, boys," said Harry. "Search and destroy. I want every single Herber scion on the planet to disappear in the next minute."

"Roger!" piped the tiny ones, and teleported themselves away.

"And meanwhile I'll fix this." Harry beamed his time-reversal ray at the hole I'd made in the side of the blunzing chamber. The giant pseudopod slid back, my sledgehammer was whole again, and the rent in the chamber's side healed over.

"It's eleven fifty-nine," said Sondra.

She pulled the magic door open. The view was as before: hyperspace below, moon robots above, microorganisms on the left, and endless hills to the right. There on the other side was our own world, seemingly upside down, and with good old Antie still waiting.

The zillions of tiny Harrys came suddenly swarming back, chattering like schoolchildren. They'd done their job: this world was clean. Tad Beat had not died in vain. The cloud of Harrys settled down on big Harry like flies on cowflop.

Somewhere a bell was tolling twelve. Time to go. Sondra and Harry grabbed me under the arms and flew me through the door.

I crashed to the floor of Harry's real workshop and shuddered with relief. The bell outside finished tolling midnight, and then the blunzing chamber was just an empty, copper-covered box.

"I can still fly!" exclaimed Sondra. Blond and shapely, she was floating in midair.

"Sure," said Harry. "It'll last a few years. I changed the quantum responsiveness of your atoms. As they're replaced, in the normal course of things, you'll slowly lose the power."

"And my money?" I couldn't help asking.

"Don't worry. It's under your bed. I suppose I could have gotten myself something too, but I guess I didn't want to."

"Don't you know what you want, Harry?"

"No. Do you? Does anyone? What's good today is bad tomorrow, and this year's disaster is next year's golden opportunity. I got what I needed—an exciting adventure. I saved that whole planet from the brain-slugs."

Suddenly I remembered the driver. "Harry, the experiment had one lasting effect you don't know about. A man jumped through to our world just before you—"

"What?"

"Yes, a man with a spine-rider. With one of the Gary-brains on his back. I wanted to stop him, but—"

"Dr. F.'s right," volunteered Antie. "A man came through the blunzing chamber just before your return. He ran out onto Suydam Street."

"Joe!" Sondra wailed. "How could you?"

"I—it wasn't my fault. Do those special guns still work, Harry?"

Harry threw his ray gun on the floor. "No, I unwished them at the end. I thought they'd be too dangerous to have around. But we've got to stop that man before his slug can reproduce! They could take over our whole world!" And then, shockingly, Harry began to laugh, first in high squeals and then in sloppy guffaws.

I stepped forward and shook him. "Don't get hysterical, Harry. Sondra! Call the police!"

"I'm not hysterical," said Harry, still chuckling a little. "I'm just excited. You're a real pal, Fletch. Who else but you would have found a way to bring Gary Herber back with us?"

"It's not a game, Harry. This isn't some wild fantasy anymore. Your superpowers are all gone! Do you have any kind of gun?"

"There's a flare ray by the cash register," said Harry, sitting down and wiping the laugh-tears from his eyes.

I found the flare ray and ran out into the street, hoping to spot that taxi driver. The sleazy New Brunswick street was empty, save for a drunk leaning against the wall outside the Terminal Bar.

"Did you see anyone go by in the last five minutes?" I demanded. "A big strong guy with round shoulders?"

The drunk gestured vaguely at the door to the bar. I braced myself and went inside. There were a few drifters and a lady of the night, but no trace of the man I was looking for.

"What'll it be?" said the bartender, a stocky man with a gray mustache.

"I'm looking for a big guy with round shoulders," I said. "He just came in here a minute ago."

The bartender favored me with a look of contempt. "He's already found his *friend* for tonight. I think they went to the john. And I'm just trying to run a decent place to drink."

"Thanks," I said, and headed for the men's room. There was a good chance I'd find two men with spine-riders in there. I held my flare ray at the ready.

But the men's room was empty. There was nothing moving except the air that swept through the open bathroom window. I jumped up on the toilet seat and wriggled out. There was an alley back there, an alley leading out to the main drag. I ran out the alley as fast as I could, but I got to the street too late. A gray car with two round-shouldered men in it was just pulling out. I chanced a shot with the flare ray, but a flare ray's not much good on plastics. The car sped off, headed toward the turnpike.

I hurried back to Harry's. Sondra was still on the phone. I yelled the gray car's license number to her and jumped into my Buick.

"Hold on, Fletch, let me come too." It was Harry.

"*You.* You think it's all a big adventure. Well, it's not, Harry. If you had children you'd understand."

But Harry got in my car anyway. He had a hunting rifle, probably his father's. I floored the gas and sped off after the gray car with the two spine-riders. Was the nightmare ever going to end?

13

Porkchop Bushes and Fritter Trees

THE gray car got away. At first I could glimpse it up ahead of us, but then I couldn't find it anymore. We tried the side streets, but the gray car was nowhere to be seen. After a while we heard sirens and saw some cop cars speed past.

"Sondra must have convinced them," Harry observed. "Why don't you just drop me off at my shop, Fletch, and then go on home to Nancy. Leave the chasing to the police."

"They don't realize what they're up against, Harry. Those Gary-brains—they could take over our world."

"Ah, look, tomorrow we'll blunze you with the rest of the gluons and you can fix everything. Don't worry so much."

"Maybe you're right. But listen, I know what it's like to have a spine-rider. It was inside my thoughts.

It's horrible." Another worry occurred to me. "The slug on my back talked to the slug that the taxi driver brought over here. So it might know where I live." I turned a corner and pulled onto Suydam Street. "What'd you think of that odalisque woman on the cushions?"

"She was nice," said Harry. "But she killed Tad. Sondra's much prettier."

"You better hope Sondra doesn't realize she's too neat for you."

"Oh, it won't sink in for a while."

I pulled up in front of Harry's shop and sat there in silence for a minute, trying to sort it all out. Sondra flew out to see what we were doing.

"I called the police," she said, leaning in my window. "But it was hard to know what to tell them."

"So what'd you say?"

"I said the two men were wireheads. I said they had stim-units on their backs and that they'd tried to rob me."

"I hope you told the cops to be real careful. If the Gary-brains take *them* over, we're really going to be hurting."

"Hey, look, Fletch," said Harry, "if you're so worried, why don't you just get blunzed right now and fix it?"

"No, no. Not now. No more craziness right now. I'm wiped out. If the brains don't spread too fast, it might be good to wait a few days to see if there's any other bad side effects coming up."

"Well, all right. Good night, Fletch. And thanks a lot. This has been a weekend to remember." Harry got out.

"Goodbye, Joe," sang Sondra, hovering next to Harry. "Say hi to Nancy for me."

"Sure thing. Talk to you tomorrow." I kept worrying as I drove back toward Princeton. How much about Harry and me did the invaders know? Wouldn't they want to come kill us as soon as possible? Or at least take us over? I drove faster.

The lights were on in my house, and the front door was unlocked. Serena was sleeping peacefully, the TV was on, but there was no Nancy. Before doing anything else I went to look under our bed— the money was there, stacks and stacks of bills. I stuffed a few thousand dollars in my pants pocket and went back out to the kitchen.

I noticed then that the back door was ajar. I was glad I'd kept Harry's flare ray.

"Nancy?" I called, sticking my head out. "Are you out there?"

"Joe! Come see!" It sounded like her mouth was full.

When I stepped out the back door I smacked into a tree that hadn't been there before. The whole yard seemed to bristle with exotic vegetation—very strange, as this morning we'd had nothing but crabgrass. I got back to my feet and spotted Nancy in a patch of light spilling from our living-room window. She was crouched down by a bush, eating something.

"What are you doing, Nancy? What's that bush?"

"It's a porkchop bush," she said, waving the greasy bone she'd been gnawing. "And there's a fritter tree right next to you! You really came through for world hunger!"

I glanced at the tree I'd bumped into. Sure

enough, there were thick bunches of golden fritters hanging from its branches. I picked one and
bit into it. The fritter was sweet and crisp on the
outside, moist and doughy in the middle. Porkchops
and fritters had been Nancy's favorite meal when
she'd been growing up in Virginia. No wonder she
was out here eating.

"But where did they come from?" I asked.

"I was lying in bed reading when all of a
sudden—it was about ten o'clock?"

"Go on."

"All of a sudden a little box popped out of
nowhere. I knew that you and Harry were up to
something, so I thought it might have jewels or
something precious in it. When I opened it, there
were just a bunch of seeds. I was in a bad mood, so
I threw them out the window and kept reading.
But then a few minutes ago I heard leaves rustling
and I came out here to see what it was. It's food
plants, Joey! It's the solution to world hunger, just
like you promised me. You're wonderful!"

"Don't you want to hear about my trip?"

"Just taste one of these porkchops!"

I felt around on the porkchop bush till I found
something fat. I snapped it off at the stem, a
perfect little porkchop, grilled to a turn. I got
myself another fritter and filled my stomach. Each
fritter had a seed like a cherry pit in its center.
The porkchops bore their seeds nestled against
their bony stems. I pocketed several seeds of each
type.

"This really *is* good, Nancy. And they grew in
just two hours?" I looked around the yard. There
were five or six of the bushes and three of the

trees. "I'm glad our trip did some good after all."

"What do you mean?"

I told Nancy about our trip to the looking-glass world, about Gary Herber, and about the parasite that had made it back to Earth. She made me show her the spot where the brain had bitten me, and she said that she hoped I wouldn't have to get blunzed. I agreed—the idea of a big needle in the skull didn't sound too appealing—and told her how I was worried the slugs might come after us tonight.

Just then Serena appeared in the back door. "Wet."

"You wet your bed, honey?"

"Bed wet."

Nancy and I went in, changed Serena, looked at our five million dollars, made sure the front door was locked, then took Serena out back for a fritter. "Taste this, Serena."

"Yes," urged Nancy. "Mommy used to like them when she was little."

Serena bit, chewed, swallowed, and approved. "More."

Just then I heard the sound I'd been half waiting for. A police siren.

"Nancy, I think that might be the slugs coming to get us. We better run."

"That's just the police, Joe."

"But they might have been taken over by Gary-brains. Quick, let's head for the woods."

"There's bugs in there, Joe, and snakes."

"Please." The siren was drawing closer.

"Oh, all right."

I picked up Serena, and we ran for the woods.

Thick and viny, the woods came right up to the edge of our housing development. It was kind of swampy in there, and the built-up land the tract houses were on sloped down at the edge. We slid down the slope and stared back at our house.

Sure enough, a motorcycle and two squad cars with flashing lights were pulling right into our driveway. Five cops with riot guns—they all had round shoulders. Serena started to ask a question; Nancy stuffed another fritter in her mouth. We crouched lower, barely daring to watch.

Bang, bang, bang. Pounding our door. One of the cops circled around to our backyard and noticed the kitchen door open. He went right in and opened the front. They stomped around in there for a while, shouting my name. I wondered if they'd gotten Harry yet. This was bad, this was very bad.

"You think they have those brains on their backs?" whispered Nancy.

"Yeah."

"What can we do?"

"Shhhhh."

One of the police cars was driving around on the grass now, shining its lights this way and that. We pressed ourselves down into the underbrush. Serena started to whimper. I got my mouth against her and whispered to her. "Be quiet, honey. The bad men are after us. Be quiet like Mommy and Daddy. Real quiet."

She obeyed. The police tried pounding on some of our neighbors' doors. No one knew where we were. An hour went by before they finally gave up. The cop with the motorcycle stayed in our house and the others all left.

"Why don't you shoot him through the window," suggested Nancy. She'd noticed my flare ray.

"Killing a cop is a pretty serious crime. If people don't understand about the Gary-brains, I could end up in jail."

"Couldn't you focus it to just kill the slug? I don't want to stay in the woods all night. The mosquitoes are eating me alive."

A plan occurred to me. "Okay, Nancy, let's try this."

A few minutes later we were at our back door. Nancy laid the sleeping Serena down under a porkchop bush. I peered in the kitchen window. There was a tired cop with a sawed-off shotgun in his lap. He had a big bump on his back under his police shirt, and he was staring blankly at the front door.

"Excuse me," I said, walking right in. "We'd better have a conference." Nancy had stuffed a lot of leaves under my shirt, so it looked as if I too had a spine-rider.

The policeman whirled and started to raise his gun.

"Take it easy," I said, smiling and walking forward. "I got my Gary-brain already." I would have been scared to chance this if I hadn't known that Nancy was right outside the window with our flare ray aimed at the cop's head. "Come on, slide your shirt up and we'll let the masters talk."

The policeman nodded and began pulling his shirt up. He had to set his gun down to do it. I came closer, pulling at my own shirt. Now the cop's back was exposed, a big, strong back with the parasitic brain nestled between the shoulder blades. I made my move.

With one swift gesture, I slid my hand up under the brain, caught hold of the soft probes where they sank into the policeman's spine, and ripped the thing free. The policeman screamed and slumped forward. The loose Gary-brain twisted and tried to sink its tendrils into my arm. Surprisingly strong, it was more than just a brain; it had muscles. I tried to fling it across the room, but couldn't get it free of my arm. It began slithering up toward my shoulder and I cried for help.

Then Nancy was in the kitchen with me. Aiming carefully, she sizzled the Gary-brain with our flare ray. It released its grip on me and fell to the floor.

"Is he going to be all right?" Nancy asked, jerking her head at the policeman. There was a raw, bloody patch on his naked back.

"I don't know." I got some water and poured it over the man's head.

He moaned a little and then sat up. "What happened?"

"You've been under the control of a mind-parasite. How did it happen?"

"I—I haven't been myself. We were chasing a gray car, and when we stopped it, Muldoon started acting funny. He stuck his head into the gray car and something happened to him. I went over to see, and the—it got me." The man broke off to stare at the dead brain on the floor. "It was one of those. They kept splitting and getting more and more of us. They must have everyone down at the station house by now. Are you Joseph Fletcher?"

"That's right. They're after me and Harry Gerber, I think."

"Gerber, yeah. Some other guys went off after him. What are we going to do, Mr. Fletcher?"

"If I can think of a way to get to Gerber, I can fix the whole thing. Right now I'm going to hide. Meanwhile, why don't you go to the state police, officer? The parasites can't have spread very far yet. Go get in touch with some higher-ups."

"But what shall I tell them?"

"We're being invaded by an alien life form. If they don't believe you, show them your back and this dead spine-rider. We don't have a minute to lose."

The policeman sped off on his motorcycle. I filled a shopping bag with money from under the bed and locked up the house. Then Nancy and Serena and I got in the Buick and took off. The main thing I wanted right now was a chance to sleep.

14

Wanted

I woke to the sound of Nancy's and Serena's voices. We were parked on a back road some fifteen miles south of Princeton. It was as far as we'd been able to come last night before falling asleep. Fortunately I'd remembered to throw some seeds out the window before dropping off, so there was a nice little stand of porkchop bushes and fritter trees right by the car. Nancy and Serena were having breakfast. I joined them.

"How much money did you bring?" Nancy asked.

"A few hundred thousand at least. Whatever's in that bag I put in the trunk. These fritters are really good."

"They sure are. If it wasn't for the Herberbrains everything would be perfect."

"Let's see how it's going." I turned on the radio.

". . . invasion," intoned a drunk-sounding newscaster. "New Brunswick has been cordoned off, with reports of alien activity in some of the surrounding areas. An unconfirmed report states that the New York Port Authority Bus Terminal in central Manhattan has been taken over by the aliens. One of the most effective weapons against them seems to be good old-fashioned alcohol. These brainlike creatures are extremely susceptible to alcohol poisoning, and all soldiers in the cordon have been put on double-grog rations. Any listeners who are near the combat zone are advised to remain intoxicated for the duration. I certainly am. Annie?"

"Thank you, Greg. Bottoms up. First reports of the invasion began trickling in last night in the wee morning hours. A number of police officers have fallen under the control of the parasites who call themselves Herberites. Their objectives at this time remain unclear, although some of the individuals under alien control have spoken of converting people to God's Laws. There is no question that these organisms are extraterrestrial in origin, although . . ."

I turned the radio back down. "Sounds like things won't get out of control. I hadn't realized that Gary is that allergic to alcohol."

"Do you think that people are going to blame you and Harry?" asked Nancy.

"Well, the brains *are* all thinking about us. So anyone who recovers—like that cop last night—is going to know we did it. Yeah, we're going to get blamed." I turned the radio back up for a minute.

". . . was caused by two eccentric scientists, Joseph Fletcher and Harry Gerber. Authorities continue to seek . . ."

"You see?" I turned the radio off entirely.

"They won't be mad at you once they find out about the porkchop bushes and the fritter trees," said Nancy soothingly.

"The government won't like free food. What about all the people who just work to get enough to eat? People with menial, subsistence-level jobs. Those people will drop out of the work force if they got some of our seeds."

"They deserve a break," said Nancy forcefully. "I think our mission is to drive all over the country giving out the seeds. And then let the seeds spread to other countries as well. We could drive to Mexico!"

"The police will be looking for this car," I observed. "And I can't just leave Harry."

"We can buy a new car. And Harry can take care of himself."

"Well, all right."

We stripped the fruit off the bushes and trees we'd planted, and got out the seeds. Each plant yielded some one hundred seeds. If we could get some helpers, it wouldn't be hard to turn one seed into one million seeds in the course of a day. A hundred times a hundred times a hundred. There was no limit to it.

We decided to leave the Buick with Alwin Bitter and get a new car. I headed back to Princeton.

Old Bitter was sitting on his porch, reading the morning paper.

"Hi," I called from the Buick. "Remember us? Joe and Nancy Fletcher?"

Bitter smiled and waved. We got out of the car and joined him on the porch.

"Have you heard all the news?" I asked him. "About the alien invasion? Didn't I tell you Harry was going to be master of space and time?"

"I don't really see the point," opined Bitter. "All for excitement, I suppose. Everyone is supposed to get drunk?"

"The brains don't like alcohol," I explained. "They have three teachings, just like you."

"I hadn't heard that."

"Yeah, they're called God's Laws. *Follow Gary, Be Clean, Teach God's Laws.*"

"A thought virus." Bitter chuckled. "A parasitic system that propagates itself. And what else did you accomplish?"

"We have special seeds," said Nancy. "Two new kinds of plants. Look." She threw a fritter-tree seed and a porkchop-bush seed off the porch. As soon as they hit the ground you could see little shoots growing up. "They make food," explained Nancy. "Joe and I want to drive all over the country and give them to poor people."

"That sounds reasonable," said Bitter. "But where will all the extra people live?"

I glanced at Nancy. She shrugged. "There's room. It's a big world."

"And the extra pollution?" probed Bitter. "What about that?"

"Look," said Nancy, "we're going to help people get enough to eat. There's no way you can argue with that."

"Who's arguing?" Bitter smiled. "What do you want from me, my blessing?"

"I just wanted to leave my car in your garage," I explained. "I think the police might be looking for me. I want to drop out of sight for a week or two."

"Do you have any money?"

"Lots."

"Give me some."

"All right."

Bitter agreed to keep our car for a thousand dollars. He took the keys and promised to put it in the big garage under the church building.

We walked down to a GM dealer's lot and bought a Corvette right off the floor. We bought it under Nancy's maiden name: Nancy Lydon. The salesman was kind of surprised to see us pay cash out of a shopping bag. But not too surprised to take the money.

Nancy wanted to drive—she said if it was in her name, then it was her car. I didn't care; I tilted back my seat and went to sleep. There was a space behind the seats big enough for Serena to roll around in.

When I woke up, the car was stopped and Nancy was talking. "Just plant these," she was saying, "and you'll have plenty to eat."

"Thank you kindly," said the thin black woman Nancy was talking to. "What kind of seeds these be?"

I sat up and looked around. We were on some crummy back road, stopped in front of a broken-down farmhouse. It was too cloudy to tell exactly what time it was, but I figured it was about noon. Nancy was talking to a frail gray-skinned woman with a large brood of children. The ground around their little house was packed bare dirt.

"Let's plant them here," proposed Nancy, scratching two holes in the clay soil. She put a seed in each, and called for water.

"Get the bucket, Cardo," said the old woman. One of her skinny sons hastened off.

"Hello," I said getting out of the car. Serena was already up, standing at Nancy's side. "We have a new kind of plant we're giving away," I explained. "They grow fritters and porkchops."

"Now that's a fib, I know," said the black woman. "Is you folks preachers?"

Cardo came back and poured water on our two seeds. The green shoots started up, and some of the children gathered around to watch. I went over and gave Serena a hug. This was more fun than working for Susan Lacey at Softech.

"It'll take about an hour, Mrs. Johnson," said Nancy. "Do you mind if we watch?"

"I don't mind. With Luther gone, I'm happy to have some grown-ups to chat with."

"Luther was your husband?"

"He say." No more information was forthcoming. Well, so what. The seeds were for everyone—nobody was going to need to fill out a form to get them. Free food. The more I thought about the idea, the more I liked it.

Mrs. Johnson's children took a liking to Serena. They showed her how to swing in their tire swing, and one of the little girls brought out a greasy rag doll for Serena to play with. The clouds broke up and let the warm autumn sun beat down. There was a horse chestnut nearby, and Serena set to work collecting shiny buckeyes.

In an hour's time the porkchop bush was the

size of a big spirea, and the fritter tree was eight feet tall. The bush had shiny reddish leaves and fat little white flowers. Bees buzzed from blossom to blossom. Now the petals dropped, and the fruits began to grow.

In another half-hour it was harvest time. I reached up and plucked the fritters, big and bright as oranges. The children gathered around for the treat, and Nancy showed them how to snap the porkchops off the bush.

"Be sure to save the seeds," I cautioned. "You can give them to your cousins."

As soon as the plants had been picked clean, they started to bloom again. There seemed to be no end to their productivity.

"Cardo," Mrs. Johnson called, "go get Emmylou and the Curtises, too. Tell them we're having a picnic."

Cardo ran off down the road, yelling with high spirits. By the time the next crop of fruit had appeared, there were twice as many people milling around the dirt yard. Someone had thought to bring Kool-Aid; I took a long drink.

A number of the kids had dropped seeds on the ground, and these were shooting up too. The more we ate, the more plants we started. And the more food there was, the more mouths there were to eat it. Pickups and big battered sedans lined both sides of the road. Nancy and Serena and I were the only white people there, but no one seemed to mind. Mrs. Johnson kept telling everyone that we'd invented the magic seeds.

"I think we can move on now, Joey," said Nancy. "It's off to a good start here."

"Okay. Can I try driving?"

"Sure."

Over the course of the next week we handed out seeds all over central Jersey. Sometimes we ventured into the towns, but mostly we stuck to the back roads. You'd be surprised how rural New Jersey can be. What with the new depression, there were plenty of folks out there who didn't have enough to eat.

After a few days they started talking about us on the radio. Some people thought the new plants had something to do with the invasion of the Gary-brains. Others thought we must be communists. The authorities in general didn't like the idea of free food. Extensive tests were conducted on our plants, but the fritters and porkchops were just what they seemed: good, wholesome food. What with people passing the seeds around, the plants had pretty well covered the state before long. The Department of Agriculture obtained a court order for our arrest. But nobody wanted to tell them where we were.

15

Welcome, Joseph Fletcher

"NANCY, I've got to go back and see about Harry." We were slowly cruising downtown Trenton, looking for people to give our seeds to. It was dusk and there was an autumn crackle in the air.

"Wait, there's an old bum." Nancy pulled over next to a man lying on a park bench. I bounced Serena on my lap while Nancy showed the man two seeds and put them in the ground next to his bench. He seemed more interested in her breasts than in the prospect of free food.

"He's heard of us," said Nancy, getting back behind the wheel. "He said some of his friends already had the seeds."

"Face it, honey, everyone in the state's going to have our seeds before long. And it's spreading to New York and Pennsylvania."

"Then we should drive down south before winter sets in. Mexico's where they really need food."

"Can't you just mail some of the seeds to your do-gooder friends? I want to get back up to New Brunswick and see how Harry's doing. Those Gary-brains may not be spreading, but who knows? Maybe they're getting ready for a big assault." The setting sun gleamed coldly on the state capitol's gold dome. Winter was just around the corner.

"Oh, all right, Joe. I'll take you up there and drop you off. Do you think it's safe to go home yet?"

"No. They're after me for helping Harry, and they're after you for the seeds. You shouldn't have told so many people your name."

"Well, I like to get a little credit, too. And they aren't really *after* us. They just want to ask us questions. I wouldn't mind answering some questions—in the proper setting."

"You mean you'd like to get on TV."

"Well, I don't see why I shouldn't. I could be on the cover of *Time* magazine, Joe. I've found the solution to world hunger."

"Can't argue with that."

We powered out of Trenton and onto the Jersey Turnpike. "I'll drop you off in New Brunswick," said Nancy, "and then I'll mail seeds to hunger contacts all over the world. And tomorrow I'll show up at the ABC studios in Manhattan."

"Fine. Meanwhile, do you think we could stop for some supper?"

"At one of those crummy turnpike restaurants?"

"Ah, why not. I'm kind of sick of porkchops and fritters."

We stopped at a Savarin. Not surprisingly, the

day's special was—porkchops and fritters. Even the merchants were getting hold of our plants now. I had soup and a salad instead. According to the radio, our fritters contained every vitamin known to man, but I still felt the lack of green veggies. Serena ordered ice cream.

As we got closer to New Brunswick, the turnpike became more and more congested. There were numerous army trucks, but what was more surprising, there were lots and lots of school buses, most of them with crosses on them. "Killeville Christian Children's Crusade," read one. "Shiloh Baptist Old Folks Home," read another. "Shekinah Glory Gospel Fellowship," "Sunshine Open Bible Network," "Women's Hope-a-Glow Ministries."

"What are all these nuts doing here?" I wondered. We reached the New Brunswick exit and crawled off amidst troop trucks and buses. The actual road into town was barricaded. An unsteady sergeant with two flares waved us toward a parking area.

"It must be that stuff about God's Laws," remarked Nancy. "People are so into religion these days."

"I can hardly believe it. They didn't say anything about this on the radio." A big light-blue bus lumbered into the space next to us. Elderly seekers began swarming out.

"I'm going to leave before someone baptizes me or something," said Nancy. "Look out for the brains, Joe. Get yourself some whiskey."

"All right, baby. And be sure to hire a good lawyer before you go on television. Just in case. There's still a lot of money in the trunk. This week has been fun, hasn't it?"

"It has. It's been like a honeymoon."

"A frittermoon. I love you, Nancy."

"I love you, Joe. Say bye to Daddy, Serena."

"Bye."

I kissed my two girls and then they drove off. I walked back to the parking-lot entrance and asked the sergeant where I could get some booze. He was a swarthy kid in his early twenties.

"There's a liquor-store someplace out that way," he said, waving one of his flares vaguely. He seemed quite drunk.

"Can I just buy some from you? I don't have a car, but I've got lots of money."

The sergeant glanced around, looking for officers. "You ain't a looter, are you?"

"No, man, I'm a tourist. Here's fifty bucks."

The sergeant pocketed my bill and handed me the flares. "I'll just be a minute."

I directed another bus into the parking area, and then the sergeant was back with a canteen full of grain alcohol.

"Government issue," he said, smiling broadly. I took a swig, retched a little, then took another.

"Thanks, sarge. This stuff keeps the brains off?"

"For sure. Gary don't like it."

"What are all these groovers doing here?" I jerked my head at a group of flower-print ladies doddering past.

"They started coming in a few days ago. The evangelicals got some idea that Gary is the new Messiah. We can't stop 'em from going in, and so far none of them has tried to get back out."

"Weird."

"You know it, brother."

I handed him back his flares and joined the throng marching toward New Brunswick. I fell into step with a pale-faced little man in a red windbreaker. It said "Virginia Beach Rescue Squad" on the back.

"Would you like a drink?" I offered.

"Praise Jesus, no," he said. His voice was sweet and reedy. "It'd be a shame to meet the Lord all messed up, now, wouldn't it?"

"The Lord's not here," I countered. "It's a bunch of brains from another dimension. They're parasites."

"Gary Herber's here," said the man stubbornly. "I seen him on TV. Gary's come to roll out the scrolls."

"What—what does Gary Herber look like?" I asked. I had a pretty good idea of what the answer would be. "Does he look sort of like a toad? A short fellow with ropy lips?"

"That's right, friend. And he has an angel with him. A blond angel what really flies. Our minister brang us up here to join salvation."

At the edge of town there was a welcoming committee, round-shouldered young men with wholesome smiles. They herded the new arrivals into a big building and—presumably—slapped Gary-slugs on everyone inside. I sidestepped this action by stuffing my sweater under my shirt and saying I was already saved. The whole scene seemed amazingly disorganized on both sides. The Herberites didn't give much more of a damn than the soldiers did. If you wanted a slug on your back, you could have one, and if you didn't want a slug, that was fine, too.

I walked up Suydam Street, wondering where I'd find Harry. His apartment seemed like the logical place to look first. He'd either be there or at the local TV station.

There were a lot of people in the street, all of them wearing brains. Despite the chill, most of them had their shirts off so that the Gary-slugs could touch each other and converse. I hung onto my canteen of booze and enjoyed staring at the women's tits. Weird to see so many of them at once.

When I was still a couple of blocks from Harry's, a cry went up from the people around me. "The angel of the Lord! Gary's angel!"

It was Sondra, stark naked and with a Gary-brain on her back. She flew about fifteen feet overhead, staring down at us with a glassy smile. I covered my face lest she recognize me.

"These are the last times!" bellowed a woman next to me. "Praise Jesus!" I took another drink and pushed my way forward. I hoped the blunzer would still work. I had to undo this madness.

The closer I got to Harry's, the denser the crowd got. It was like Mardi Gras—except everyone was high on slug-stim instead of booze. Some zealot ripped my shirt off, exposing my naked back. Herberites rubbed up against me so their spine-riders could split onto me, but by now I had enough booze in my system to be unpalatable.

"Follow Gary!" chanted the crowd. "Be Clean! Teach God's Laws! Follow Gary! Be . . ."

So far they'd been totally nonviolent, but I was getting more and more nervous. I kept pushing forward, smiling a lot, and occasionally splashing a little alcohol on my back. It was hard to see why the army didn't move in and clean up this mess. I guess they were too drunk.

Finally I was in front of Gerber Cybernetics. There were some guys guarding the door. One of them was really big. I lurched forward and made my request. "Can I go in? I'm an old friend of Harry Gerber's."

"Thou art not saved," stated the big black-haired guard, frowning down at my naked back. He looked vaguely familiar.

"I'm a mystic," I said ingratiatingly. "I love you people too."

"What is thy name?"

"Joe Fletcher."

"Behold!" exclaimed the guard. My name seemed to mean something to him. "It's the prophet's herdsman who hath fed the kine. Welcome, Joseph Fletcher!"

"WELCOME, JOSEPH FLETCHER!" roared the crowd behind me.

I couldn't resist turning to bow and wave. And then the guards let me in.

"Dr. F.," said Antie, hurrying forward, "I'm so glad to see you. I don't know what's gotten into all these people. My Harry's not been himself."

"Where is he?"

"Upstairs in the throne room."

"Throne room?"

"He gets sillier every day."

I followed Antie upstairs. Sure enough, the dining table had some rugs and a chair on top of it. This was Harry's *cathedra*. To my relief he was pacing around the table instead of sitting on it. He had his shirt off, and he wore a huge brain in the center of his back. Aside from Antie, we were all alone.

"Grab him, Antie, it's for his own good."

"Check, Dr. F."

Before Harry could say anything, Antie had him in a double hammerlock. Moving quickly, I poured a half pint of booze over the the big brain on Harry's spine. Shocked by the poison's contact, the brain drew itself together. I slid my hand under it and pried it loose like I'd done with the policeman's Gary-brain. The heavy alien plopped to the floor.

"Stomp it, Antie."

She did.

16
Blue Gluons

"WOOD," groaned Harry. He was leaning on the dining table and shaking his head. "I feel like everything's made of wood. God, and you stomped my poor brain, Antie? Help me, Fletcher, I'm hurting bad."

"You want a drink?" I handed him the canteen. Harry tilted it up and worked his throat for a while.

"Plastic," he sighed, finally lowering the canteen. "At least now everything's plastic."

"How long have you been under Gary's control?"

"Ever since the night we came back. The brains got Sondra and me while we were sleeping. What day is it today?"

"Monday again. It's been a week."

"Time goes fast when you're having fun." Harry twisted his head around, trying to get a look at his back. "Did it leave much of a mark?"

"I'll get a bandage," volunteered Antie. "And some germ cream. Don't worry, Harry dear." She bustled off to the kitchen.

"I—I was on TV," said Harry. "Sondra and I were sort of starting a religion."

"Sort of? You've seen the crowds outside, haven't you?"

Harry laughed and shuddered at the same time. "It's perfect, isn't it? It just goes to show that everything I've ever said about religion is true. The sky's the limit when it comes to religious stupidity. Here we have a race of alien invaders, and the evangelical true believers are flocking here to get taken over. And meanwhile—"

"Before you get too snotty, Harry, just remember that you're their leader. Did you like wearing the brain?"

Harry shrugged, finished my canteen, and padded out to the kitchen for more. We passed a bottle of Scotch back and forth while Antie bandaged the raw spot between Harry's shoulders.

"Sure I liked it," said Harry finally. "You've been through it. There's the constant nerve stimulation, and even more important, there's the feeling of working for a larger whole. Normally I never have any real reason for the things I do. Believing in Gary felt good." Harry fell silent for a moment, then went on: "What's the public reaction to all this? Aside from my—followers, I mean."

"I don't know, it's kind of weird. The army's got New Brunswick surrounded, but they don't seem ready to move in. Last week everyone was very excited about the invasion but now—now they're all talking about the food plants. Since the Gary-brains aren't doing much of anything, people have sort of lost interest."

"Food plants? You mean those seeds I made for Nancy?"

"That's right. Porkchop bushes and fritter trees. Nancy and I have been handing out the seeds all over the place. That's one wish that really seems to have worked out well. But speaking of wishes, what about Sondra? I saw her flying around naked outside. We should try to get the slug off her back."

"My angel," said Harry in maudlin tones. The booze was hitting him hard. "My poor fallen angel."

"Do you know where she is?"

"She—roosts here with me at night. In my bedroom."

"So Antie and I will get her slug off when she comes back. Or maybe I should get blunzed and make all the Gary-brains disappear at once?"

"I used the rest of the gluons up," muttered Harry. He seemed to be having trouble staying awake. "And it didn't work, did it, Antie?" He pushed off from the counter he'd been leaning against and lurched across the room. "Need to lie down. Look out for Sondra."

Antie and I stretched Harry out on his bed and prepared to ambush Sondra. Holding a big tumbler of straight booze, I stood pressed against the wall next to the window like a forties gangster listening to the cops outside. Antie stood against the wall on the window's other side. We passed the time by chatting a little about the past week's events.

Apparently Harry and Sondra had tried to crank the blunzer up again. Gary wanted the door to his universe reopened so that some of him could go back there. And he'd wanted a few changes made in our world as well: slugs everywhere, a centralized dictatorship, no booze, et cetera. Antie and Sondra had run through the sequence just like before, but when the hotshot table jabbed Harry, nothing had happened.

"I was glad," said Antie. "I think Gary would have gotten rid of all the robots too."

"Did you sabotage the blunzer, Antie? Is that why it didn't work?"

"No, no, I was scared to. Last time it almost killed me, you remember? There were still enough red gluons, but they just didn't work."

Suddenly I remembered something. The strangely familiar voice I'd heard on my car radio when I'd been in the infinite regress in the Softech parking lot that last Friday after work. *The red gluons only work once,* the voice had said. *Use blue gluons the second time.* Blue gluons? I wondered if Stars 'n' Bars would have them. Could the voice on the radio have been my own? Perhaps I was destined to take my turn as master of space and time.

The sound of wild cheering snapped me out of my reverie. The crowd outside was really getting excited. Peeking out the window's corner, I could see that most of the people had taken off all their clothes. They were writhing around with all the Gary-brains splitting and sliding from back to back. I guess you would call it an orgy. And hovering above the worshipers was their queen: Sondra Tupperware, lovely as Marilyn Monroe, weightless as a cloud, naked as a wet dream.

"She'll come any minute now," said Antie. I took

a little taste from the glass I was holding. Harry's steady snoring filled the room.

Finally the yelling outside came to a peak—it sounded like everyone climaxing at once—and our blond angel came floating in through Harry's open window.

I scored a bull's-eye with the glassful of booze. Before Sondra could even peep, we had the Gary-brain off her back and under Antie's metal feet.

"Joe!" she exclaimed, covering her breasts. "What are you doing here?" Then she noticed that her breasts weren't all there was to cover. She dove for the closet and found herself a robe.

"You better let Antie put a bandage on your back," I suggested. "If modesty doesn't forbid."

"Oh, Joe, I've . . ." She stepped over to the bed and felt Harry's empty back. "How long have we been—"

"It's been a week. They got you the first night back. They came for me and Nancy, but we got away."

"Was that whiskey you threw on my back?"

"That's right. Gary's allergic to it, remember?"

"I—I'd better have a drink. And some food. The spine-riders don't bother to feed their hosts very often."

There wasn't much of anything in the fridge—Antie said the stores were almost out of fresh food—but there were a few things in the freezer. Antie microwaved Sondra some fried chicken with mashed potatoes, and I poured her a big glass of white wine.

"I want to use the blunzer," I told her.

"It doesn't work," said Sondra. "Thank God."

"I think you just had the wrong kind of gluons," I explained. "Harry told me once that gluons come in three colors: red, yellow, and blue. I have a hunch that each color just works once."

"You mean the blunzer will work exactly three times?"

"Just like in all the fairy tales. I think it's about time for our second round of wishes."

"You'll get rid of the Gary-brains?"

"Don't you think I should?"

Sondra pulled the oversize bathrobe tighter around herself. "Yes, of course. Though the people they're attracting are so stupid that—"

"They're better off this way? That's a thought. Maybe that's why the army is letting them keep coming in. Anyone who'd volunteer for alien domination doesn't really deserve to have his or her freedom. It's a thought, Sondra."

"But this is still just stage one. As soon as people stop coming to New Brunswick, the Gary-brains want to break out."

"You know that for a fact?"

"Didn't Harry tell you?"

"He didn't say much of anything before he passed out. You better get some sleep too, Sondra. I'm going to need your help tomorrow."

"I'm scared." She poured herself another glass of wine. "I'm scared the brains will come back while I'm sleeping. Will you get in bed with me, Joe?"

"What a question! Have you looked in a mirror lately?"

"Oh, don't be like that. Underneath, I'm still

plain Sondra, you know. I wish I could get my real face back."

"Tomorrow. Tomorrow we'll get some blue gluons and I'll fix everything up. Why don't you finish that wine and then we'll go to bed."

"Okay, Joe."

17

Sit on My Butt

THE phone woke me up. It was just getting light outside. I had a Type III hangover: wavy jello and cold pain. The phone was next to our bed.

"Hello?"

"Joey! You're all right?" It was Nancy.

"Yeah. Yeah, baby, I'm fine. Are you in New York?"

"That's right. I called the network and I'm going to be on the Brad Kurtow show this morning. I'm staying at the Plaza Hotel."

"Class. I'm sleeping in a double bed with Harry and Sondra. I got the brains off their backs, and today I'm going to try and get blunzed."

"What do you mean you're in bed with Sondra?"

"Just to protect her, Nancy."

"Well, let her protect herself, that blond cow."

"It's not her fault she looks boss. As a matter of

fact, she wants me to change her back to the way she was."

"You're really going to get blunzed?"

"I think so. I'll get rid of the Gary-brains and—I don't know. Is there anything else I should wish for?"

"Get us a penthouse on top of the Plaza, Joey. I like it here."

"Anything else?"

"I want to be able to fly, too. Like Sondra. Why should she get everything? I'll flit in and out of our penthouse like a dove."

"That sounds nice. And I'll wish for ten million more bucks while I'm at it."

"And immortality?"

"No, no. I don't want to live forever. Death's the only thing that keeps me going."

"Well, don't forget the other things. Good luck, darling. I have to catch a cab now."

I set the phone back down on its cradle and felt around on the floor for the Scotch. Normally I don't drink in the morning, but today I had a good excuse. Several of them.

The taste of the stuff made me cough and retch so loud that it woke the others.

"Wood," groaned Harry. "Everything's cheap splintery beige and white—"

I handed him the bottle.

"*I* don't have to drink that, do I?" asked Sondra.

"Not really," I said, taking another hit. "You and me will be flying out of here before any brains can bother you. You'll be able to carry me, won't you?"

"Sure she can carry you," said Harry. "She's

been flying me to the TV studio every day. It's her atoms—they're all made of null matter in EPR synchronicity with her state of mind."

"What does that mean?"

"My body moves whichever way I will it too," said Sondra. "If you sit on my butt I can fly you anyplace."

"We need to get to Stars 'n' Bars," I said, trying not to think too hard about Sondra's butt. How would it feel to have a body like that?' "I want to get some blue gluons."

"McCormack won't have them," said Harry. "They're much harder to isolate then the red ones are. What do you need blue gluons for anyway? You planning to play scientist?"

"Antie told me you tried using the red ones again and it didn't work. I was thinking maybe there's some sort of exclusion principle: each color of gluon will work once in this universe, and that's it."

"Fermi statistics," said Harry musingly. "It makes a sort of sense. But blue gluons, Fletch? I doubt if there's more than two or three grams of them in the whole world. And guess who has them?"

"Someone we know?"

"You remember Professor Baumgard?"

"Oh, God. Him?" Dana Baumgard was a big-time establishment physicist who'd hated Harry and me for years. The feud had started when we beat out his lab for a weapons contract—it was for a special beam that would make the enemy's water supplies radioactive. What made Baumgard so mad was that although Harry and I had put together a working model, we'd been unable to explain how or why it worked. As far as Baumgard was concerned, I was a sleazy carnival barker and Harry a dangerous, tinkering geek. I didn't look forward to visiting him.

"Where's the professor these days?"

"He's the head of the Super Intersecting Proton Loop out in Iowa. SIPL is the only facility in the country that can reach the energies needed to produce blue gluons."

"*Iowa?*"

"It's nice and flat. Makes it easier to build the loop, which is in the shape of a figure eight, ten kilometers long. One loop of the eight holds protons, and the other loop holds antiprotons. The particles circle and circle around their loops till they get up to speed and then someone throws a switch to make the two beams collide."

"Can you fly me all the way to Iowa, Sondra?"

"Can't you take a plane, Joe?"

"You can do it, Sondra," said Harry, sitting up on the edge of the bed. "I'll build you an electronic windfoil."

"Joe has to promise to change my body back if he manages to get blunzed." Sondra was trying to scoot out of the bed without having her robe flap open. "I'm tired of everyone staring at me all the time."

"Anything you want, Sondra. I'll get breakfast while you get dressed." I went into the kitchen and got some stuff out of the freezer. Ham steaks and frozen waffles. Antie set to work heating them up. "I'm going down to my workshop," called Harry. "I want to build that windfoil for you two."

"Hold on," I shouted, hurrying out into the hall.

I could hear some of the guards moving around downstairs. I grabbed Harry and put my lips to his ear. "Put something under your clothes so they think you still have a spine-rider. Otherwise—"

"Gotcha," murmured Harry. He rummaged in the hall closet and found a small knapsack to wear under his sweater. There were a lot of pretty dresses in the closet; apparently the spine-riders had let Sondra do some clothes shopping. I reached into the closet and touched the prettiest dress of all: a red-and-white-candy-striped number.

"I'll be right back," said Harry. He clattered downstairs and called a bright hello to the guards.

Sondra stepped out of the bedroom, looking great in tight jeans and a frilly white top. I reminded myself to stop staring at her.

By the time we'd finished breakfast, Harry was done with the windfoil. It was a little box with a parabolic antenna on top. The box was supposed to generate a kind of special ray that would force the wind to streamline around us instead of beating our faces. Harry showed me how to turn it on and adjust its dials.

"Where exactly in Iowa *is* the SIPL?" I thought to ask.

"Just north of Ames. Follow I-80 west to Des Moines and turn right—you can't miss it."

"And what happens when Baumgard refuses to sell me the gluons?"

"You kill him." Harry handed me a sawed-off shotgun and a handful of shells. "You blow his stinking head off."

"But, Harry—"

"That's *illegal*," chimed in Sondra. "We'll go to jail!"

"Listen," said Harry, grinning and holding up his hand for silence. "This morning Fletch the thief kills Baumgard—big trouble. But this afternoon Fletch the master of space and time resurrects Baumgard—*non habeas corpus*! No body, no crime."

I couldn't stop myself from chuckling. What a plan!

"Well, I guess so," said Sondra. She turned and walked into the bedroom. She bellied down across the bed, her face toward the open window. "Come on, Joe. Sit on my butt."

I sat on her butt. It was big and hard, but not *too* hard. Once again I caught myself wishing that I could have such a beautiful body myself. I pocketed the shells and put the shotgun and the windfoil in my lap.

I was on Sondra like a rider on a horse. To fit through the window I had to crouch down like a jockey in the stretch, but then we were out over the street. It was raining. The Herberites cheered when they saw us; they must not have noticed that our backs were flat.

We followed the Raritan River out of New Brunswick. There were troops on most of the bridges; some idiot even took a shot at us. We gained altitude and headed west.

The wind was starting to tug at my face now, and the rain was hurting my eyes. Gripping Sondra's waist with my knees, I sat up and adjusted the windfoil. I diddled the knobs until an invisible energy net reached out in front of us to wedge a break in the wind and rain.

"Isn't this great, Sondra?"

"Yeah, I really love to fly. It's been a lifelong dream of mine. Could you stop squeezing me so hard? If you do fall off, I can always catch you."

"Oh. Sorry." I let up on the knee pressure, and Sondra angled upwards. Now that the wind had stopped, there really wasn't much danger of slipping off. "When I change your body back to looking the old way, you still want to be able to fly, right?"

"That's right. That's what I wanted in the first place."

We were up above the clouds now, and the air was clear and cool. The hot morning sun beat on my back. Now and then through a rent in the clouds I could see Pennsylvania. The trees had all turned red and yellow. From the air, the wrinkled hills looked like rucked-up carpet. Then came flat Ohio, scuzz Great Lakes, and checkerboard Indiana.

"*I-o-way!*" I shouted as we crossed the Mississippi. "I've never been here before."

"I have," said Sondra wearily. "And I hadn't planned to come back."

18
Why Things Exist

THE Super Intersecting Proton Loop looked like some primitive earthwork: a giant figure eight in the midst of empty cornfields. There was a glass and metal building where the rings intersected. We touched down in a field nearby.

"When were you in Iowa before?" I asked Sondra.

"In the fifth grade. My father took some horticulture courses at Iowa State so he could grow better marijuana. But then they expelled him for not paying any bills. We lived in the married-student housing in Ames. Quonset huts. It was a long time ago." She stumbled on a cornstalk and caught my arm. "Don't you think you ought to hide that shotgun?"

"Right." After checking that the safety was on, I slid the barrel of the gun down under my waistband and pulled my shirt over the stock. I set the electronic windfoil down at the edge of the corn-field.

Though it was only about nine in the morning, Iowa time, Baumgard was in his office. For a moment he didn't recognize me.

"I'm Joe Fletcher, Professor Baumgard. Harry Gerber's friend?"

"Oh, Lord. Fletcher and Gerber again. I hear that you two are responsible for those mind-parasites invading New Jersey. I don't suppose you can tell me how you did it?"

The guy was a real square. He had long, greasy gray hair and a beard. A microcomputer in the pouch of his sweatshirt. And—*ugh*—Beatles music playing softly on his radio.

"I can try." I started to tell him about the blunzing chamber and the way the vortex coil could churn the gluons into Planck juice and . . .

"That's enough, Mr. Fletcher. That's *quite* enough gibberish for today."

"Our machine worked, didn't it?" My voice was rising. Baumgard really knew how to get under my skin.

"How should I know if your machine works or not. I don't even know what it's supposed to do."

"It grants wishes. Look at *her*. Harry gave her the power of flight." I pointed to Sondra, who'd been standing quietly to one side. "This is Sondra Tupperware, by the way. She's a minister in the Church of Scientific Mysticism. Could you float in the air, Sondra?"

Sondra hovered halfway between floor and ceiling. Baumgard looked away in disgust. "Have you come here simply to show me your parlor tricks, Mr. Fletcher? Have you brought a deck of cards as well?"

"No," I said, trying to control my voice. "I've come to ask for your help in stopping the alien invasion."

"Oh, my. How exciting. Why doesn't Gerber reinvent his inertia-winder and fly the bad monsters away?" Baumgard was referring to a sort of rocket drive that Harry had come up with a few years back. Somehow we'd forgotten how to build it—the conclusion of the affair was a little hazy in my mind—and we'd ended up losing a lot of money.

"I need some blue gluons, Professor Baumgard. Give them to me and I'll make your dreams come true."

Baumgard leaned back in his chair and laughed. "Make my dreams come true. You should work in a carnival, Fletcher. You should be the barker for a freak show." Abruptly the savant stopped laughing. "And I'm asking you to leave. Must I call Security?"

It was time to get out the shotgun. I turned away, maneuvered the gun from under my clothes, then spun back to level the short barrels at Baumgard's face. "Harry says that if I kill you now, we can probably bring you back to life with the blunzer. You want to try it?"

"You'll never get away with this, Fletcher."

"Where have I heard that line before?"

"You'd better give Joe the blue gluons," Sondra piped up. "I think he wants an excuse to kill you."

That wasn't true at all, but Baumgard seemed to believe it. The guy really had a low opinion of me.

Just thinking about it made me wish I had an excuse to kill him.

But now he'd unlocked one of his cupboards and he was getting out a little magnetic bottle. "There are three and a third grams of blue gluons in here."

Still keeping the gun aimed at him, I unscrewed the bottle's lid and glanced in. Ink, sky, sea, my heart. It was the genuine article. "What do you want for it?" I asked, tightening the lid back on. "You can have anything you want, Professor Baumgard."

He tried to tighten his face into an ironic smile, but he couldn't quite pull it off. Whether he liked it or not, he knew there was a chance I could deliver.

"I'd—I'd like to understand the universe," said Baumgard huskily. "I'd like to know why things exist and what matter really is. I'd like to understand how things can be the way they are." For a moment there was a childlike hunger on his face. "Take the gluons. I'll give you ten minutes and then I'll call the police."

"Thanks. That's more than fair. I'll do what I can for your wish. You might have your answer by tonight."

"Sure I will, Colonel Fletcher." All at once Baumgard's voice had turned high and sarcastic. He regretted having bared his soul. "I'll look for the answer right next to the two-headed calf and the half-man half-woman. Say hello to your geek friend for me."

Sondra and I hurried out of Baumgard's glass and metal building, picked up the windfoil, and took off. We didn't talk much till we stopped at a McDonald's in Geneseo, Indiana, for lunch.

"I liked his questions," said Sondra, biting into a Big Mac. "Those are good, heavy mystical questions. Why do things exist? How can things be the way they are?" Men all over the restaurant were staring at Sondra, but I'd gotten used enough to her appearance to be able to focus on what she was saying. She tore open a catsup and squeezed it onto her fries. "I didn't realize that a groover like Baumgard could think about questions like that."

"Yeah, the guy's not all bad. I just hope I'll be able to make the right wishes for everyone. Old Bitter sure wasn't much help when I asked him."

"Do you remember what he said?"

"First he turned the question back at me. I'd asked what I should wish for if I was master of space and time. And Bitter replied, 'What does God have in mind when He makes the world?' Then he said that this world was just fine."

"*This* world? With Gary-brains and fritter trees?"

"I mean the old world, the way it was before Harry made his wishes. Though this *is* the same world, really. It's just later in time."

"What about the looking-glass world?"

"All the worlds are part of our superworld. But, like Baumgard asks, why do these things exist? Why is there something instead of nothing?"

"It *is* nothing," protested Sondra. "That's enlightenment, noticing that nothing exists. And then not noticing."

"God." I sucked hungrily at the bottom of my Coke. "What the hell are we talking about anymore?"

Sondra laughed and sipped her coffee. "How long will you be blunzed, Joe?"

"He just gave me three and a half grams. When Harry took a hundred grams, it lasted two hours. So my trip should last a thirtieth of that. Four minutes."

"That's not much time."

"I'll make a list to make sure I do all the right wishes. I have to send my voice back to my car ten days ago, and eliminate the Garys, change your body, and Nancy wants a bunch of stuff too. And there's Baumgard's answer, and I want some more money."

"Money? That's all you care about?"

"Well, God, at least you can count it. And you don't have to decide how to use it right away. I'm going to ask for ten million dollars."

"It's counterfeit money, though, isn't it, Joe?"

"You call this counterfeit?" I pulled out a crumpled twenty and handed it across the table. "It's flawless."

"But money has to come from somewhere, Joe. It's supposed to stand for something that someone did. Caught a fish, made a shoe, told a story."

"Well, I'll say I stole blue gluons and shot them into my head. And that I made wishes for a lot of people. I call that doing something." In my excitement my voice had risen again. Everyone in the place was staring at Sondra and me. Our conversation and appearance were kind of unusual for Geneseo, Indiana.

There were two college kids at the table next to us, a bearded fat boy and a pimply girl with glasses. The girl was staring at me so hard that she didn't notice when my eyes met hers. It was as though she were watching television.

"Can we have some wishes too?" asked the boy. He smiled to show that *he* was kidding if *we* were.

"No way," I snapped. "I got my hands full already."

"Don't be like that," Sondra reprimanded. "Charity cleanses the heart." She shot the beard a Monroe tooth dazzler of a smile. Her lips, her dimples, her spit. *Oh, Sondra,* I thought, *I'd give anything to look like you.*

"I think," said the beard in his wet, nerdy voice, "I think I'd like some marijuana ice cream."

"Yeah, yeah, yeah," said his date, tittering and rocking back and forth in her seat. "With cocaine whipped cream."

"And an LSD cherry," whispered the boy.

"Beautiful," I said, getting to my feet. "Mellow." Other people were pressing toward us. I had half a mind to unlimber the shotgun and commit Midwest mass murder. I didn't like for strangers to make fun of me and rip me off at the same time. "You coming, Sondra?"

"When I'm ready." She took out a little pad of paper and licked her pencil. "Can you two give me your addresses? Joe will send you each a special cone. Won't you, Joe?"

There was a state trooper sitting at a table not too far away. He was looking at us like he'd heard the drug words. If it kept up much longer, I figured to shoot him first.

"Sure, Sondra. Anything you say. Give her your addresses, kids."

"You first," said the boy to the girl.

"No, you."

"You tell."

"You."

Somehow we finally got out of Indiana.

19
I Wish I Had a Wish

THE clouds over Jersey had cleared off, and I could get a good look at the countryside. Unlike those in Pennsylvania, most of the Jersey trees and bushes were still green. At first I thought they must all be pines, but then a chilling thought hit me. The porkchop bushes and fritter trees had taken over!

"Could you fly a little lower, Sondra? I want to see something."

"Okay."

Sure enough, the trees were heavy with orange fruit, and the bushes were greasy with meat. These mutant plants seemed to actually be undermining the other vegetation; as I watched, a stately elm tottered and crashed to the forest floor. The fritter trees had eaten its roots.

"What are those big plants?" Sondra asked. "Are those the food trees you were talking about?

"Yeah. Let's land and take a look."

The porkchop-bush thickets were so dense that we couldn't reach the ground. Instead we perched in the fork of a two-hundred-foot fritter tree. From below you could hear the porkchop bushes growing—they made a steady rustling. In the distance, a mighty oak went crashing down.

"Like kudzu," said Sondra. "The vine that ate Dixie."

"Kudzu?"

"It's a Japanese vine they brought into the South to stop erosion. It stopped the erosion, but pretty soon it covered all the other plants up. Not really *all* of them, but—"

"Well, these things *are* killing all the other plants. They're tearing down the other trees and eating them!"

"It's really out of control," said Sondra. "You feel how this tree is growing?"

Indeed, our tree was lifting us upward like a slow-motion Jack's beanstalk. Peering down through the leaves, I saw a deer that had been strangled by a porkchop bush's runners.

"These things are going to take over the whole planet!"

"Looks like you've got another wish to make, Joe."

"Oh, brother. Nancy's going to be sore about hunger. Nothing is working out the way it was supposed to. You see now why I just ask for money? It's the only safe wish."

I remounted Sondra and we flew back up into the sky. Here and there were a few remaining patches of real trees, but the green stain of the mutant food plants was spreading steadily. A few isolated farmhouses had been taken over as well. I wondered if the farmers had been able to escape.

New Brunswick looked the same. Troops all around it, and the streets full of Herberites. We whisked in through Harry's bedroom window and hurried down the hall.

Harry was passed out at the kitchen table, his face in a plateful of candied yams. Antie was busy keeping Harry's followers from coming up to visit the throne room.

"Our leader is meditating," she called down the stairs to them. "He is receiving truth."

"Looks like he received a whole fifth's worth."

"Oh, Dr. F., I'm so glad you're back. Those vulgarians keep asking for Harry."

"We'd better pour some water on him. I'm going to need his help to get the blunzer going."

"You found the blue gluons?"

"Yes," said Sondra. "And we didn't have to shoot anyone."

"Thank goodness."

Sondra and I drank a little vodka to keep the Gary-brains off, and then I got to work.

"Harry," I crooned, dribbling a glass of water over his scalp. "Wood, Harry. Wooden thoughts, wooden moods, wooden sensations." I reached down and began pinching his cheek. "Dry martinis, Harry. Cold beer. Fried chicken. Naked women. Come on, you fat slob, wake up!"

Slowly he righted himself. There was a big orange smear of yam around his mouth. "Those brains," said the mouth. "They won't get me again."

"I have the gluons, Harry. Three and a third grams."

"Four minutes' worth," he said, brightening. "Do you know what to wish for?" He dabbed daintily at his mouth with a filthy handkerchief. "I seem to have dropped off for a minute."

"Here, Harry," said Antie, proffering a mug of sweet coffee. "Drink this to clear your head." Harry slurped down the coffee while Sondra and I knocked back a little more vodka.

Finally our leader lurched to his feet. "Let's do it."

"What about the disciples?" fretted Sondra. "They'll smell the liquor and try to—"

"Fletch'll kill them," said Harry. "Did he waste Baumgard?"

"I don't kill anyone," I protested. "I'm no gunsel."

"Then give me the shotgun. Lead the way, Antie."

Antie told the disciples to leave, but one of them wouldn't budge. It was the big fellow I'd spoken to yesterday, the jerk with the stained-glass vocabulary. Suddenly I realized where I'd seen him before. He was the chauffeur who'd carried the first Gary-brain over here!

"Behold," he intoned, walking toward us with open arms. "The flesh of our Lord's udder hath been milked to anoint the Father's wen."

"Beat it," snapped Harry. "Or I'll blow your stinking head off."

"He *likes* that expression," whispered Sondra with a giggle.

"But, master, surely it is written that the oxen low. And where His hoof hath sucked . . ."

The shotgun blast was very loud in the small

store. Fortunately Harry was so ripped that only a few pellets struck his looking-glass disciple. The fellow took off like a whipped dog. A lot of people pressed their faces against the store window to peer in. Antie locked the front door.

"We better go in back," I urged, taking Harry by the arm. He was trying to reload the shotgun. I had the gluons in one hand. "Come on, Harry, don't antagonize them."

"It is the Anti-Gary," the big disciple was wailing outside. "His milk is sour!" An angry mutter swept through the crowded street. The people looking in the window could see we had no slugs on our backs. Harry was leaning over now, trying to pick up a shell he'd dropped.

"Goddamn, Harry, come on!"

Sondra and I dragged him back into the workshop. Antie had already started the blunzing chamber's refrigeration unit.

"Okay, Fletcher," said Harry. He was suddenly sober. "Give me the gluons and go on in there. Just lie down on the hotshot table and put on the breathing mask."

With difficulty I made myself hand Harry the bottle of gluons. I couldn't believe it was already time for me to get blunzed. I hadn't even made up my list of wishes. But the crowd outside was increasingly noisy. Someone was hammering at the back door. They'd be breaking in before long.

"Does the needle hurt much?" I wanted to know.

"Turning chicken?" snarled Harry as he clicked on the microwave cavity. "Would you like me to get blunzed instead of you?"

"Don't let Harry go again," cried Sondra. "It has

to be you, Joe. You're the only one with enough sense."

"All right," I sighed. "But I wish I had something I really wanted. I wish I had a wish."

"Maybe you'll think of something," said Sondra soothingly. "I'll try to help you." Lord, she was beautiful.

"Antie, get the gluons," said Harry. "Well, go on, Fletch. Go on in."

The street noise had grown to a steady roar. I opened the blunzing chamber's door and peered in at the grim death table. Flakes of frost formed in the frigid air.

"Is there anything you want, Harry? Any wishes for you?"

"Just get Gary Herber off people's backs. I've had enough excitement for a while."

"Don't forget about me," called Sondra. "Or the fritter trees."

There was a crash from the store's front. They'd broken the big window.

"Here goes," I said, and hurried into the blunzing chamber. It was cold and dark. I lay down on the hotshot table and slipped the breathing mask over my mouth. Sondra slammed the door shut, and then one of them energized the chamber's copper sheathing. The electrostatic field set most of my hair on end. As my eyes adjusted to the dark, I could see faint glow-discharges at the tips of my fingers.

Now came the singing sound of the gluons merging into the microwave field, and then the crash blast of the gluons being fed into the vortex coil. There were yelling voices in the workshop—the

Herberites. Harry's shotgun roared; the voices drew back.

The vortex coil grew louder, so loud that the struggle was drowned out. The hotshot table shook with the chatter scream. I braced myself for the instant when the long needle would plunge down through my skull.

There was a heavy thump. Agony in my ears, chamber at vacuum, the swift crunch of needle through bone. I tried not to scream.

The Planck juice was in my brain now, I could feel the white heat of it. My whole body felt prickly and soft. I was a hologram made of pure light.

The needle slid back out. I sat up. Copies of me twisted off like soap bubbles from a bubble wand. It was still dark in the blunzing chamber. I could see perfectly. I felt no need to breathe. A crowd of tiny Fletchers flew around me. My little echoes, correction terms to the blunzing process. This felt good. This felt good.

I wished myself out of the chamber, and there I was, out in the workshop. A terrible fight was in full progress. Five of the Herberites had broken in. Harry had killed the big looking-glass one with his shotgun, but just now one of the others had slashed Harry's throat open with a machete! Covered with blood, Harry was lying dead on the floor!

Seeing me, Sondra began screaming for help while the Herberites with the machete charged at me and . . .

I WISH EVERYTHING BUT ME WOULD STOP MOVING. The trick for stopping the world is basically to turn your time axis at right angles to everyone else's. It's nothing for the master of space and time.

The room around me grew still. The struggling people were like so many waxworks.

I WANT A DIGITAL DISPLAY OF THE TIME I HAVE LEFT. Purple numbers appeared in my field of vision: *3:50*. Only ten seconds gone so far. Good. Now what? First bring Harry back to life—he'd done the same for Antie.

I glanced over at Harry—but that's not quite correct. I could see in every direction at once, all the time. When I say, "I glanced over at Harry," what I really mean is that I focused part of my attention on him. A few hundred of the little Fletchers flew over to transmit my wish. I healed up his wound, and as an afterthought, got rid of his headache. Now it was time for the real work. Too bad I'd had to hurry into this half-cocked.

3:42.

I WISH I HAD MY LIST OF WISHES.

20
God Goes Trans-Sex

1. Send voice back.
2. Sondra's body.
3. The Gary-brains.
4. Ten million dollars.
5. Plaza penthouse.
6. Power of flight for Nancy.
7. Porkchop bushes and fritter trees.
8. Indiana.
9. Baumgard.
10. How the blunzer works. Tell Harry.

THE list, in my own handwriting, seemed to be complete. I tucked it in my shirt pocket and got to work.

As I've mentioned, I was able to see in every direction at once. More than this, I was also able to see through any obstacles. In ordinary vision, what one does is to combine various two-dimensional retinal impressions to build up a three-dimensional mental image. But now that I was master of space and time, the whole world around me was somehow contained in my head. I could see everything that everyone was doing.

But this was not all. By a slight effort, I was able to see not only the present world but also the worlds of the past. Normally such an influx of information would be staggering, but to me it was as pleasant as the sea is to a fish. It was no trouble at all to fix my attention on my Buick in the Softech parking lot, ten days ago. I could see the little images of Harry on the dashboard, and I watched as he warped my past self into a doubly infinite regress. When my past self turned on the radio, it took only a touch of my volition to make the circuits speak my piece. I didn't need to send my body back like Harry had. It sufficed to send my will.

"THE RED GLUONS ONLY WORK ONCE," I informed my past self. "USE BLUE GLUONS THE SECOND TIME."

A bit more chitchat and my first task was done. Sondra's body was next on the list. By keeping part of my attention on the past I was able to use her original body as a model. I turned her hair back to a kinky brown, flattened out the proud mounds of her breasts, thickened here and thinned there. End of second task.

3:10.

Now the Gary-brains. Here the little Fletchers

came in handy. Just as Harry had done, I sent my little echoes out into the world around me to seek out and disintegrate each Herber-brain they found. As an additional precaution, I teleported the five Herberites back out into the street. I didn't want them to attack on sheer momentum when I reentered their timestream. My little helpers came flying back—all the aliens had been destroyed.

2:50.

The Plaza penthouse was the hardest wish yet. First I had to find Nancy and read her mind for the plans. Rapidly I scanned all over Manhattan till I found her. She was—I was surprised to learn—in a jail cell downtown. They'd busted her at the studio. I sent the thumb-sized Fletcher to reassure her and look into her mind. Once I could see what she wanted, I had to will the penthouse into existence—furnishings and all. And on top of that I had to create the paper that went with: titles, deeds, variances, and tax records. Not only did I have to create them but I needed to place them in the proper bureaucratic file cabinets. When I finally had the thing done, I plucked Nancy out of jail and moved her into our new home. For the finishing touch, I plopped ten thousand thousand-dollar bills down in front of her. Whew!

1:45.

Over a minute I'd wasted on that! What else did I still have to wish for? My mind seized up in panic. I got out my little list. Five down, five to go. Next was *Power of flight for Nancy.*

I didn't quite understand how Harry had gone about giving Sondra the power of flight. I recalled him saying that he'd done it by turning her atoms into "null matter in EPR synchronicity with her state of mind," which may or may not have meant something. Instead of trying to think it through, I just looked back in time and copied the mind-state that Harry had when he did it. Holding the strange, Gerberesque thought pattern steady, I applied it to Nancy's body. Good.

Now for those food plants.

My tiny echomen came in handy again. I sent the endless flock of them out to scour the planet for porkchop bushes and fritter trees. This took some doing, as Nancy had mailed the seeds far and wide. That was what she'd been arrested for, apparently: a slew of customs violations. I found and destroyed all the documents relating to her case while my echomen repaired all the damage the plants had done. What next?

Indiana. Get serious. Those stupid kids could just . . . I stopped myself. It behooves a god to be merciful. I located them and shoved the desired drug confection into each of their stupid faces.

Baumgard. That was the really tough one. I was a lot more powerful than I'd ever been, but I wasn't really much smarter. What had he asked to know? *Why do things exist?*

1:25.

I tried looking into the future in hopes of finding a book with the knowledge Baumgard sought. But the future was not accessible to me. As far as I could tell, it didn't really exist. Trying to see into the future was like looking at a page of movie ads. Lots of pictures, but no way to be sure which one you're going to visit. *Why do things exist?*

Instead of looking forward, I tried peering back

through the eons. There were the dinosaurs—I sought till I found some small mammals, our ancestors. Before that, the great empty seas—I brought some molecules together into a double helix. Further back. Great disks of dust slowly clumping into planets and stars. I nudged them to make the lumps show better. But I needed to look much further, back to the very start!

My vision shook with the effort. I held to the task. Back, back, back through the billions of years. Almost at the start now. Space filled with radiation, utterly symmetrical. *The symmetry has to break,* I thought, and made it happen. Further.

Energy-filled space. So small, so big. Earlier. Where did it come from? *Why do things exist?* Someone had to put it there. But who?

I focused all my energy on the initial moment of our universe. I drew strength from all the space and time around me, and funneled raw existence back to—make our universe begin.

Why do things exist? Because I created this universe. Baumgard wasn't going to like the answer. *:38.*

There was a tenth item on the list: *How the blunzer works. Tell Harry.* I didn't recall having wanted to make any wishes like this. But better do it. I still had time.

I stared at the blunzer next to me and let myself merge into the essence of its workings. Then I flipped back through time to feel its action as it blunzed me, and earlier, Harry. I understood it then, I understood it totally. But I couldn't quite put my understanding into words.

With part of me still in the past, I reached out to

the resuscitated Harry on the floor next to me and read the physics terminology off the wrinkles of his brain. Now I had it. Now I really knew how the blunzer worked.

But there was still one last part to the tenth wish. *Tell Harry.* Why tell him when he already knew? The answer hit me like a ton of bricks. Harry hadn't always known how to build a blunzer. When I'd asked him on that Saturday how he figured it out, he'd told me he got the the idea in a dream. A dream he'd had the night before.

I scrambled back to the night of Friday, September 21. As I'd been doing all along, I sent only my consciousness, *not* my whole body. Harry's whole song and dance about having to send your body back and send a lizard forward was easily avoidable. My will could reach back in time and do whatever was needed.

My immaterial eye found Harry peacefully asleep in his double bed. Plain Sondra was next to him, snuggled against the soft curve of his fat back. I'd come to the right place, but how was I to get into Harry's dream?

It was easy. I reached into his mind as before, but this time I did more than observe his thoughts. I altered them. I set up a feedback loop between my thoughts and his; it felt as if I'd stepped right into his dream.

In the dream, Harry is sitting by a river with a beautiful girl. She is his anima, a projection of subconscious goodness. They have a picnic basket, and they are throwing all their food into the river. A duck is eating the food—a strange duck that walks on the surface of the water.

"Harry," I said, tapping him on the shoulder.

He gave a hoarse cry of surprise, and the anima disappeared. "What are you doing here, Fletcher?"

"I've only got a few seconds. I've come to tell you how to build the blunzer."

The duck and the river had disappeared now, too. Still in the dream, Harry and I were sitting face to face at a long table. In the space of an instant, I took everything I knew about the blunzer and coded it onto Harry's brain.

:10, read the clock. I snapped back to my body in Harry's workshop. I tried to understand everything I'd just done, but it was too much for me now. I twisted my time line back parallel to the world's. The people in the room with me started moving again.

:09.

Harry felt his throat gingerly, then sat up and grinned up at me. "Thanks, Fletch. I needed that."

:08.

"Oh, Joe," exclaimed Sondra, looking down at her flat body, "it's perfect."

:07.

Seeing Sondra so dull and plain again really bothered me. I could still see into the past, and I feasted my eyes one last time on the way she'd been.

:06.

At the same time I looked over my list again, making sure I hadn't left anything out. I had a feeling there was one more wish I wanted.

:05.

Sondra and Harry didn't realize I'd been out of

their time for four minutes. They thought I was just beginning. I could see it in their minds.

:04.

"Don't you have any deep, hidden desires you're going to ask for?" Sondra was saying.

:03.

Suddenly I realized what my real wish was.

:02.

"I WANT TO BE A BEAUTIFUL WOMAN!" I cried. "I WANT TO LOOK JUST LIKE SONDRA DID."

:01.

The numbers disappeared. My field of vision narrowed back down to what it had been. Something was hanging in front of one of my eyes. I reached up to touch it.

Long, blond hair.

21

Men Are People Too

"WHAT a homo!" exclaimed Harry once again. "I can't believe it."

I ignored him and continued to stare down at my new body. I still had on the same clothes as before. "If you don't mind, Harry, I'd like to go to the bathroom."

"I bet you would. Can I watch?"

"Forget it. I'm happily married."

"Do you know where we can reach Nancy?" Sondra asked.

"She's in a penthouse on top of the Plaza Hotel. Call the operator, it's a new listing. Or just wait a minute. I can tell her myself."

I walked out of the workshop and up the stairs to Harry's apartment. The bathroom was right off his bedroom. I was eager to look myself over in privacy. I was having trouble grasping what I'd done.

As I passed the bedroom window, I looked out to see how the stupid groovers were doing. Still shirtless, most of them, but all their Gary-brains were gone. Thrown back on their own limited mental resources, the zealots didn't seem to have much to say for themselves.

I locked the bathroom door and took all my clothes off. It was a nightmare, a dream come true. I was a woman as beautiful as Marilyn Monroe. I pressed my hands between my legs. My big breasts slid this way and that, jiggling with every motion. My hips and butt stuck out like shelves.

I was horrified, yet of course I was thrilled as well. Whatever regrets my conscious mind may have had, my subconscious was in ecstasy. I got into the shower and soaped myself all over, getting to know my new body.

Someone knocked on the door as I was toweling myself off.

"Who's there?" My voice was sweet and melodious.

"It's Sondra, Joe. Do you want one of my dresses?"

"Yes, thanks. That candy-striped one? And a bra and stockings."

"Unlock the door."

"Okay."

I held the towel up over myself while Sondra brought in her new clothes for me. They fit perfectly. Acting like a friendly sister, she showed me how to put on lipstick and mascara.

My new face didn't look *exactly* like Sondra's had. Somehow you could vaguely tell that it was still Fletcher.

"I want heels, too," I said, brushing out my long

hair. "I might as well do the whole number. And can you give me a little handbag with some money in it?"

"Joe—"

"Call me JoJo."

"JoJo, what are you going to do now?"

"Get the train to New York. I want to look at our new penthouse."

"I called Nancy, JoJo. She's pretty upset."

"Oh, she'll be glad to see me."

"I'm not so sure."

I left Harry's shop soon after—it embarrassed me to try to talk to him while I looked like this—and walked down to the train station. Now that the invasion was over, I figured the passenger trains to New York would be stopping in New Brunswick again.

My heels—shiny red ones—were a little tricky to manipulate, but I found that if I walked slow and swayed a lot it wasn't too hard. The volunteer Herberites in the street seemed pretty disoriented; most of them were drifting back out to the parking lots at the edge of town. The men all stared at me, of course. I was careful not to meet their eyes. This quickly became a real drag—having always to look at the sidewalk or the rooftops—but I certainly didn't want some ugly bristly man to try to pick me up.

This probably takes a little explaining. You'd think that any man who wants to be a woman is basically homosexual. But—at least on the surface—this didn't seem to be true for me. My wanting to look like the blond Sondra was really a heterosexual impulse: the craving for a supreme merging with the object of desire. But what was I going to do now—spend all my time looking in mirrors and taking showers? More and more, I was realizing how badly I'd blown it.

There was quite a crowd of people up on the train station platform, most of them just regular citizens happy to be free of the slugs. The station-master assured me that a train for New York would be stopping in twenty minutes. I sat down on a bench outside the waiting room.

"Hi," said a man, sitting down next to me. He was nicely dressed and had a polite expression. "I'm sure glad those naked brains are gone."

"Me too," I said. "I hope things will go back to normal now. The mutant plants are gone, too, aren't they?"

"That's right. Those guys Fletcher and Gerber are really going to get it."

"Uh ..." I tried to cover my confusion. I'd forgotten about that angle. As long as the Gary-brains had run New Brunswick, Harry had been safe from the authorities. But now ...

"Would you like a cigarette?" He drew out a pack of menthols and offered me one.

"Thanks," I said, accepting the cigarette and a light. His fingers brushed against my hand.

"My name's Brad. I'm a stockbroker in the city."

"I'm JoJo. I—I'm starting a new life."

"You don't have a husband?"

"No, but—"

"I'm surprised someone as gorgeous as you isn't married. Are you a model?" Brad smiled at me, his eyes flickering over my voluptuous curves. "I love your dress."

"Oh, I was in computers." I felt increasingly flustered.

"Brainy, too!" Brad grinned and slapped his face in mock astonishment. "Look, JoJo, I know this is kind of sudden, but I'm going to be leaving the office at five, and if you'd like to have dinner—"

"No, no!" I squeaked. "I couldn't possibly."

"Tomorrow, then?"

Some cigarette smoke went down the wrong way and I went into a coughing fit.

Brad watched, smiling patiently. As far as he was concerned, anything I did was wonderful. "Can I get you some water, JoJo? A Coke?"

"No, I'm afraid I—" I lurched to my feet and gave him a smile. "I have to go."

"Well, all right. Another time, maybe. I'll be looking for you."

Feeling suddenly unsteady on my heels, I teetered into the waiting room. It was three-thirty. Ten more minutes until the train. I went and hid in the ladies' room.

The train, as it turned out, was filled with state troopers. They had come to make sure New Brunswick was really secure. Watching them get out, I realized that one of their first tasks was going to be the raiding of 501 Suydam Street, home of the mad scientist Harry Gerber. For the moment I was glad not to look like Joe Fletcher.

Fortunately my admirer didn't get in the same train car as I. I plumped myself down next to a cute brown-haired woman with big glasses. Her clothes were kind of tattered.

"Isn't it wonderful to be able to leave New

Brunswick?" she said to me. "I feel like the last week has been a long bad dream."

"Do you live here?" I asked, ready for some pleasant girl talk.

"No, I was just visiting my boyfriend at Rutgers. He's a graduate student in engineering. My roommates must think I've been killed!"

"Yes," I said. "It's been awful. Did the aliens make you do anything that—"

"I don't want to think about it," the brunette exclaimed. "And all those rednecks showing up. I'm going to see my gynecologist as soon as possible. I bet they got after you too, what with your figure and blond hair."

"Yes," I lied. "Gary Herber made me go out in the streets at night. With the brains sliding around and everyone grabbing each other—"

"Men are so awful," said the woman next to me, her face momentarily close to tears. "Those brains were like men, the way they glue onto us and try to use us. Even my Tommy's like that, a little bit."

"Men are people too," I protested. "They just want to be happy like women do."

"Don't kid yourself, sister." My companion's voice took on a hard edge. "Men and women don't want the same things at all. When's the last time any man did something really romantic for you—without wanting to get paid back the same night?"

"You have to think about the genes," I said. I'd heard a theory about this. "Basically all a person wants is to perpetuate his or her genes. The best strategy for men is to have lots of children with lots of different women. The best strategy for women is have children and make sure the father stays around to help take care of them."

"Ha!" snapped the woman next to me. "Some man must have told you that. *All a person wants is to perpetuate their genes.* Boy, is that stupid."

"Well, yes," I said after a time. "I guess it is."

I got a taxi at Penn Station. "The Plaza Hotel," I told the driver.

"Sure thing, little lady."

I sat back and watched the buildings sweep past. People, people, people. And all of them thinking, all of them just as conscious as me. When I'd been a kid I'd always thought of grown-ups as a race apart—big meat robots, really. Then once, when I was in my twenties, my father had said something funny to me. We were playing golf behind a four-some of businessmen in colored trousers and billed caps.

"Look at them, Joe," my father had said. "They really look like they know what they're doing. I'd always thought I'd be like them someday. I'd always thought I'd get to be a grown-up. But I'm not. I still don't feel any different. I'm sixty and I still don't know what I'm doing."

As the years passed, I'd come to understand what my father meant. Even though I was almost forty, I still didn't feel like a grown-up. I didn't really feel much different from how I had in high school.

And now in the taxi I was thinking that the same thing is true for men and women. As a man I'd always assumed that women are somehow not like real people. Of course I never put it that baldly, but the feeling had been there all along.

Yet now here I was, with the tits and ass and lipstick—still just a person. The woman on the train—I'd never quite talked to a woman that way before, without the sex game somewhere in the background. As she'd unselfconsciously told me about her boyfriend and her job and her roommates, I realized something that I'd only seen in flashes before.

Everyone is just a person trying to be happy. Everyone is really alive.

What a liberation to know this! What a burden!

22
Strictly from Detroit

"Do you expect me to have sex with you?"

"Well, sure. I'd rather do it with you than with anyone else."

"The way I feel now, Joe, I'd rather do it with anyone else *but* you. How could you pull this on me?" She paced back and forth across the enormous living room. Outside the big French windows lay the wonderful clutter of Manhattan. "We could have been so happy." There were tears in her eyes.

"Come here, Nancy. Come sit on the couch with me."

"No. And you killed the fritter trees, too."

"They were taking over. You know that. That's what you got arrested for: distributing dangerous, nonapproved seeds."

"I suppose the police will be coming for me again?"

"I don't think so. I repaired the damages, and I erased all the documents relating to your case. With no documents and no more fritter trees or porkchop bushes, I don't see how—"

Someone was pounding on the door. It was the police, two of them.

"Hello, ladies," said the older of the two. He was a white-haired man with a weathered face. "Is this the residence of Joseph Fletcher?"

"Yes," said Nancy. "But—"

"He's not here," I interrupted, getting up from the couch and swiveling over to the cops.

"Do you mind if we take a look around?" asked the old cop, giving me an appreciative once-over. "You see, we have a warrant for his arrest."

"Come on in, boys," I cooed. Nancy look disgusted. I winked at her and sat back down on the couch. I was too tired to stay standing.

The police left after a while, and Nancy finally came over to sit next to me. The sun was going down. I wished we could go to bed, but I knew better than to suggest it. We held hands and the silence deepened.

"I could have you declared dead," Nancy said after a while. "And then remarry."

"You can not," I snapped, letting go of her hand. "Joseph Fletcher may be missing, but without a corpse he's not legally dead."

"Serena needs a father."

"Where is Serena, anyway?"

"I left her with Sybil Bitter."

"Alwin Bitter's wife?"

"That's right. I went back down to Princeton

before coming to New York. My TV interview was really exciting, Joe, you should have seen it." As the room darkened, Nancy was finding it easier to talk to me. "They arrested me right on the Brad Kurtow show. I was in jail all day, and then suddenly I saw this thumb-sized little man who looked like you."

"That was me, all right. An echo of me."

"And then I was here in this wonderful penthouse. I still haven't looked at all of it yet. And I can fly, Joe. I've only tried it a little but—"

"Would you take me flying with you now? It's dark and no one will see us. We could fly over to the World Trade Center and back."

"But you can't fly, can you, Joe?"

"I can ride on your back. I did it with Sondra."

"Well . . . take that silly dress off first."

In the bedroom there was a dresser that looked like mine. The top drawer was filled with money—Nancy had stored all our money in here for me. The other drawers were filled with Joseph Fletcher clothes. I selected a pair of corduroys and a flannel shirt. Stepping into the bathroom, I noticed a pair of scissors. I took them and cropped my long hair short. Then I used a washcloth to get the makeup off my face.

Nancy was in the living room, hovering above the floor. She smiled when she saw me, appreciative of the gesture I'd made

"That's much better, Joe. You look almost like your old self. I was just thinking—with all our money, maybe you could get surgery to . . . you know . . ."

She flew down and hugged me. "Oh, Joe, why did you do it?"

I gave a quick shrug. "A subconscious desire. I've always wanted to be a beautiful woman."

"Me too," laughed Nancy.

"But you are."

"Not the kind that drops men in their tracks. I thought those policemen were going to pass out when they saw you."

"Hey, let's go flying. If you really want me to be dead, you can just drop me on Times Square."

"You'd make quite a splash."

We opened a big French window and flew out into the night. Nancy's wiry body felt nice between my soft thighs. The cool air beat against us as the staggering city perspectives swept past. We looped around the Empire State Building, zoomed along a cable of the Brooklyn Bridge, and finally alighted on the flat top of one of the twin towers of the World Trade Center.

"You fly well, Nancy."

She closed her eyes and let me kiss her. The kiss felt just like it always had.

"Are you still my same Joe?" said Nancy after a while.

"I'm still the same. I'm still the same inside."

"Then let's go back. Let's go back to our new house and try to be happy together."

I'd like to be able to say that we had a steamy night of all-girl sex, but it didn't work out that way. I ended up sleeping on the couch. When it came right down to it, Nancy couldn't face the thought of me sleeping with her. Ever again.

The morning TV news was bad, too. Harry Gerber had been arrested and charged with criminal negligence in the deaths of seventeen people who had died of shock when the slugs got them in New Brunswick. His laboratory was under heavy police guard, and Sondra Tupperware had been arrested as an accessory. Joseph Fletcher was still being sought, but charges against Nancy Lydon Fletcher had been dropped. All the mutant food plants had disappeared, and their depredations had been undone. Some scientists speculated that perhaps the fritter trees had been a kind of mass hallucination brought on by the Gary-brains.

Someone was pounding on our door again. Nancy was still asleep. I went to look through the peephole. Newsmen, with video cameras.

"Go away," I fluted. "I don't want to see anyone."

"Please, Mrs. Fletcher," shouted back the reporters. "Just a few questions."

I went to the phone and called Security. After a while the noise at our door died down. Nancy was up now, and I made us breakfast.

"Sooner or later, one of them's going to talk," I said over the eggs.

"Who?"

"Sondra and Harry. Sooner or later they'll tell the police that I've turned into a woman. And then I'll get arrested, too."

"Arrested for what?"

"It was on the news. Seventeen people died from having the spine-riders on them, and they're charging Harry with criminal negligence. Sondra and I are supposed to be accessories. And I bet Professor Baumgard is going to charge me with armed robbery."

"You'd better call Don Stuart. The lawyer I hired yesterday."

"Oh, lawyers . . . There must be a better way to fix all this. Don Stuart isn't going to give me back my sausage, is he?"

"Well, with plastic surgery—"

"I want my *real* body back. This just won't do. I want to have more children with you, Nancy. And I want poor Harry out of jail."

"What about Sondra?"

"Oh, she'll get out. The first time they put her in an exercise yard, she'll fly away. If they hand-cuff her to a guard, she'll just take the guard with her. You don't have to worry about Sondra, Nancy. It's just Harry and me that are getting screwed."

"Not literally, I hope." Nancy smiled and ruffled my spiky hair. As long as we weren't in the bed-room she felt able to act affectionate.

We took our coffee out on the terrace and stared down into the chunked canyons of Manhattan. This was really a neat place to live. If only . . .

"Why don't you use the blunzer again?" asked Nancy suddenly.

"Didn't I tell you about the red and blue gluons?"

"Yes, but you said there were yellow gluons, too. If you find some yellow gluons, then the blunzer should work one last time, shouldn't it?"

"It's a thought. But I don't think anyone has yellow gluons. They're even rarer than the blue ones. If I could only talk to Harry—"

"Well, you can. Find out where he's locked up and go visit him. No one'll recognize you."

"They don't let just anyone off the street come visit killers, Nancy. I'd have to be a relative."

"So get a fake ID. Say you're his sister. Does he have a sister?"

"Yes! I've heard him talk about her. Sister Susie. She lives in Detroit."

"Good. That means she's not likely to be here yet."

"Right. But where do we get a fake ID?"

"You're the criminal, Joe, not me."

"All I can think of is Eddie Match." Eddie was an old friend of ours who lived way uptown. He made a generally honest living as a photographer, but he did know a lot of criminals. I'd heard him talk about forging IDs. "Let's take a cab uptown to see Eddie."

"Okay. Wait here while I get dressed."

"Can't I watch?"

"No."

She went in the bedroom and closed the door. I really hoped we'd find those yellow gluons today. It had been uncool to use a gun on Baumgard. This time I'd use money. I found a big purse in the hall closet and stuffed it with a little over two million dollars' worth of thousand-dollar bills.

Nancy was still dressing. I decided to phone up Alwin Bitter to see how little Serena was doing. His wife answered the phone.

"Hello, Mrs. Bitter?"

"Yes."

"This is . . ." In sudden panic, I realized I didn't know how to finish the sentence. "How's Serena?" I blurted.

"Serena is fine. Who am I speaking to, please?"
I hung up.

I had on my Joe Fletcher clothes from last night.
I looked in the hall mirror and wondered whether
to put on makeup. Just because Nancy was so
uptight didn't mean I couldn't get a little fun out
of my new body. My hair was a real mess.

"Hey, Nancy," I called.

"Hold your horses, I'm not ready yet," she
shouted through the closed bedroom door.

"I'll be downstairs in the beauty salon."

I left before she could protest. I'd spent my
whole life waiting for women to finish dressing;
now it was my turn to get back.

The hairdresser was chic and in his twenties.
He cluck-clucked over the way I'd butchered my
hair.

"Whatever possessed you, dear?"

"I—I thought someone would like me better
with short hair. Can you fix it up?"

"Of course, dear. He'll love the new you."

"*She*. Not too much off the sides and make it
spiky on top."

They did my hair and nails, and then they fixed
my face. I told the makeup girl I wanted to look
like I was from Detroit. She got the picture. When
they were done, I looked even better than I had
yesterday. Except for the clothes. I wondered if I
should go back upstairs and . . .

"Come on, Joe," said Nancy, stomping into the
beauty salon. "I've been waiting and waiting for
you."

We hit the street and caught a cab. Nancy didn't

want to get our Corvette out of the hotel garage. On the way uptown we stopped to buy me a tailored tweed suit in earth tones. I was starting to look kind of butch. But from Detroit, strictly from Detroit.

23
Way Uptown

"OPEN up, Eddie." I could see his eye staring out the peephole in his steel-covered door. "It's Joe and Nancy Fletcher."

"You're not Joe Fletcher." His voice was slow and amused. He was kind of a wirehead. "If I let you in, will you—"

"Here," said Nancy, pushing me aside. "You recognize me, don't you, Eddie?"

"Who's your girlfriend? Does she like men?"

"Open the goddamn door, Eddie!" I could hear someone coming up the stairs after us. This was a terrible place to be standing around with two million bucks in my purse.

Eddie let us in just as the footsteps reached our landing. Instead of a mugger, it was a neighbor, a young professional like Ed. I wondered where all the weirdos I'd seen outside lived. What a crowd!

Wireheads, she-males, black'n'whites, oz-drippers, and God's own number of gunjy mues.

Eddie ushered us down his long hall and into the living room. His two big dogs were barking.

"Tasp?" he offered, holding up a little machine the size of a flashlight. It was a remote stim-unit: if you beamed it at the base of your skull you'd get colors and a pleasure flush. Usually I didn't indulge, but right now I really needed a lift. Nancy had been cold-shouldering me ever since the beauty parlor. She'd waited in the cab—fuming—while I'd visited the dress shop. I guess it was all kind of freaking her out. *She's just a person too,* I reminded myself as I raised the tasp to my head. *A person who wants to be happy.*

I pressed the button and things got better real fast.

"What's your name?" Eddie was saying, smiling at me and holding out his hand for the little pleasure machine.

"It's Joe, Eddie, it really is." Nancy refused Eddie's offer of the tasp and kept talking. She was here to do business. "Yesterday he was Marilyn Monroe and today he wants to be Susan Gerber. We want for you to make him some ID."

Eddie zapped himself again and wandered over to the window. "Come here, Joe, look at this." Now that Nancy had confirmed it, he didn't seem to have any trouble accepting my changed appearance. He'd been living uptown for a long time. "Look at those dead cars," said Eddie.

I tasped myself once more and looked down at the cars Eddie was talking about. There were three of them on his block, cars with headlights, tires, chrome, and engine parts all gone.

"Picked clean," I chuckled.

"Check," said Eddie. "I'm always looking at them and thinking about valet parking. A salesman from Iowa, right? He leaves his car with the valet at the Sheraton, and this is how the car looks the next day. The one up at the corner was mine." He was laughing so hard now that he had to lean on the windowsill for support. "What'd you say your name was? How'd you get in here, anyway?"

"I came with her." I jerked my head at Nancy.

"Oh, right. Joe Fletcher. So you went trans-sex?"

"Yeah, basically. And I need ID. Susan Gerber from Detroit."

"Check. Hold on to this and don't let me have it back till I finish." Eddie passed me the tasp. At least he didn't have a socket yet. Once you got the socket in your skull you were pretty well done for.

"Nancy and Joe," said Eddie, sitting down at his desk. "Wow. Would you throw me that tasp, Joe?"

"You just told me not to."

"Check." Eddie turned on the desk's screen and put his fingers on the keyboard. "Susan Gerber from Detroit? Got a street address?"

"You'll have to look it up."

"Okay." He punched a few buttons and got the information. "105 Madius Street. You got a picture of the lovely new you, Joe?"

"No."

"Okay we'll do that next." Eddie hit some more buttons and the screen displayed three different ID cards, front and back. The thing had a typesetting program built in. Another push of the button and a hard copy of the cards slid out onto the desk. "Now we get the pictures and paste these up. Could you just hand me that tasp?"

"*I'll* take the tasp," said Nancy, snatching it out of my hand.

I followed Eddie into his photo room and we got the shots. He had a videoscan still camera, so there was no waiting for the prints. I studied one of the pictures, trying to believe it was really me. I was still light-headed from the stim, and it all seemed pretty exciting.

"I could do with one more pulse," I told Nancy as we came back into the living room.

"Check," said Eddie. "Me too."

With both of us standing over her, Nancy gave in. We each took a couple more pulses before she got the tasp back from us.

"Where were we?" Eddie asked.

"IDs," nagged Nancy. "If you guys are going to keep getting blasted, you could at least offer me a drink or something, Eddie."

"A beer?"

"Fine."

While Eddie was getting the beer, Nancy took the opportunity to chew me out. "You're going to go right down the drain in a hurry, Joe, if you don't get your real body back. It's not like you to be using stim this way."

"What do you care? You don't love me."

"I do too love you, Joe. Who else would put up with you?"

"I'm not so hard to get along with. I'm just a person who wants to be happy. A person just like you."

"That's your big insight from having a woman's body?"

"It's true, isn't it?"

"As far as it goes. But the surest way to be unhappy is try to be happy all the time."

"That sounds like something your father told you. What a redneck."

"At least he has a penis."

"I'm going to see Harry, Nancy. I'm going to see Harry for the gluons today."

Eddie returned with three beers. "ID," he said, reminding himself. "We still have to do the hard part." He had full-color paper replicas of each of the three cards, front and back, made out to Susan Gerber and with my picture on each one. "First, sign these, Joe. Michigan driver's license, federal citizen card, and a cash key."

"Write *Susan Gerber*," Nancy reminded me, as if I didn't know.

I signed the flimsy papers, and then Eddie took them down the hall. The dogs started barking again.

"Come on, girls," called Eddie, "I'll show you my machine."

"Which one?" I asked cautiously.

"Look." He had a plastics molder and—most important of all—a selection of official plastic blanks. If your card didn't have the right field patterns, you could forget it. The fields were like invisible seals of validation. One by one he laminated the graphics onto the plastic blanks.

"Did we talk money yet?" Eddie inquired.

"Whatever you say." I took the fresh IDs and admired the craftsmanship.

"Call it five thousand."

"Check." I took out my wad and peeled off the bills.

"Can I have my tasp back now, Nancy?"

"Sure," said Nancy, handing it over.

Eddie and I passed the tasp back and forth for a while. Pretty soon I was laughing harder than I'd ever laughed before. And then I was in a taxi again. Robot driver. There was a person next to me. Nancy.

"Where are we, Nancy?"

"We're going to Rahway. *You* are. I'll get out there and fly to Princeton. I want to get Serena."

"Check."

"Stop acting like a wirehead or I'll leave you flat."

I clammed up and looked out the window. Ugly, ugly. It seemed stupidly wasteful to take a taxi all this distance. But we had money to burn. Can money buy happiness? It still seemed worth a try. I wondered how much a tasp would cost—in case this yellow gluons thing didn't work out.

24

Spacetime Plumbers

"My cell window's right next to a metal roof, and all day there's a bumblebee out there. He's beautiful, Susie, he's just like a comic-strip bug: a big dot for a body and a lazy eight for wings. He's always patrolling his territory, you know, going around in a sort of polygonal path, but if he sees another bug—*zow!*" Harry threw his hands in the air, trying to show how fast the bumblebee could move.

"I'm not really your sister," I hissed, "I'm Fletcher! We've got something important to discuss." We were sitting at either side of a long table with an armed prison guard at the end. The guard looked too bored to be listening to us—but that could have been an act. Harry chose to ignore my whispers.

"So what I've been doing, Susie, is tricking the

bumblebee. I wad up a piece of toilet paper and throw it out through my bars. *Zoom*, he's right on top of it. I did it a lot a lot a lot until he started getting mad. He figured out where all the fake bugs were coming from."

"Please, Harry." I leaned forward, trying to get his attention. "You have to help me find some yellow gluons."

"Then I filled up my mouth with water. For squirting. Because I knew the bumblebee was going to come for me the next time I threw out a piece of paper. And he did! I tell you, Susie, he looked as big—as big as a dog, coming at me like that."

"Did you get him?" I sighed. Harry may or may not have known it was me, but right now he needed to be talking to his sister.

"I sure did. Remember those great water-gun fights we used to have with the neighbors?"

"You mean the Fletcher kids? Joe and Nancy?"

Harry shot me a look of understanding. "That's right. We had three special guns, remember?"

"I sure do. I wish I had one of them now. I wish I had a lot of things. Oh, Harry, I hate looking like this. I didn't know what I was doing."

"I wish I could help you. I'm not too crazy about being in jail, either. The feds keep grilling me, but I haven't told them anything. One of the FBI guys told me I'm going to get twenty years."

"Wow. I've got money, you know. I'll get you the best lawyer."

"Gee, thanks. You want to hear about the cockroach under my bed?"

"Come off it, Harry." We were both leaning across the table, with our faces almost touching.

The guard was definitely not paying attention any more. "I want to try running the blunzer again. Where can I find yellow gluons?"

"I've been racking my brain. Someone at Princeton might have some. Do you know any of the physics guys?"

"Alwin Bitter!"

"Beautiful. But do you think you can operate the blunzer? You don't really understand how it works, Joe."

I felt like laughing in his face. "*I* don't understand? I happen to be the one who told *you* how to build it, Harry."

His face clouded over in sudden anger. "*You?* Don't try to hog the credit, Fletcher. I designed and built it. It's my invention."

"Sure it is," I sneered. "Where did you get the original idea though, huh?"

"In—in a dream. But it was *my* dream, and—"

"It wasn't ·your dream, Harry. I fed it to you. When I got blunzed yesterday I went back in time and gave you the dream about how to build the blunzer." Harry was shaking his head and holding his eyes squeezed shut. "It's true, Harry. Remember the river with the duck that walked on water?"

Harry's eyes snapped open. "Oh. Oh, my. Didn't you have to trade some mass to move back like that? The way I had to move Zeke forward to go see you in the car?"

"I just sent my image. You don't really have to trade mass. You just did it that way so you could make a Godzilla."

"This is confusing." Harry glanced over at the guard. The guy was out on his feet. "Assuming

Bitter gets you the gluons, what are you going to wish for this time? You'll only have a second or two."

"I'd just like things back the way they were. Of course I'll keep my money."

Harry studied my face for a minute. "You're still the same underneath, Fletch. You're the one who's really crazy. That's what I always tell people, but they never listen. Have you gotten laid yet?"

"I'm scared to."

"What about the answer to why things exist? Weren't you going to find that out for Baumgard? You rushed off so fast yesterday that I never got to ask you."

"You didn't have to keep calling me a homo."

"Well, face it, Joe, anyone who—"

"I don't want to talk about it. I'll tell you about Baumgard's question. Why things exist. What I did was to look way, way back in time to try to see how it all started."

"How far back?" Harry's eyes widened with interest.

"I went all the way back to the Big Bang."

"And?"

"I caused it."

"You caused the Big Bang?"

"It was like nothing was happening and I got impatient. I was spread out all over space and time, so I just took energy from all over and focused it back on the starting point."

Harry's eyes glazed over in thought. "The universe as a self-excited system," he said slowly. "I like it. It makes sense."

"So in a way I'm God, aren't I?"

Harry gave me a look of mingled pity and amusement. "Sure you are, Joe."

"Well, look, if I was the one who—"

"*I*. Who invented the blunzer? Nobody did, Fletch, it invented itself. It came out of no place and told us how to make it. I put the parts together, you got the shot . . . Can't you see it was just using us? The universe was using us to help excite itself. There's probably lots of these sort of drains where energy gets fed back through time. We're the guys who help hook up the pipes, is all. Spacetime Plumbers."

We'd been talking too loud. The guard was paying attention again.

"I guess I'd better be going," I said, leaning back in my chair. "It certainly was nice to see you again, brother Harry. Though it's a shame it had to be like this."

"Well, Sis, God works in mysterious ways."

They processed me back out of prison. It took half an hour. So many doors, so many walls. Nancy had flown on ahead, but our robot taxi was still waiting for me. The meter was up to seventy-two dollars.

On the turnpike I tried to think through the course of events thus far. I felt like making notes. It had all started on Friday afternoon, September 20. I felt in my pockets for pen and paper and, finding none, asked the driver for writing utensils.

"Lllookkk in the storage comparrtment," the machine intoned. I turned around and snapped up the lid on the storage compartment behind my seat. It held a first-aid kit, some cans of food, a flashlight, and a type-screen. The type-screen was like a child's slate, with a keyboard at one end. You could type onto the screen and, if necessary, produce hard copies. I set the thing on my knee and made a list.

Friday	9/20	I see Harry in Buick. Harry dreams he sees me.
Saturday	9/21	We shop Stars 'n' Bars. Godzilla.
Sunday	9/22	Go to church. Harry blunzed. Trip to Looking-Glass World.
Monday	9/23	Gary-brains invade. Start trip with Nancy.
****************		
Monday	9/30	End trip with Nancy. Slugs in New Brunswick.
Tuesday	10/1	Fly to Iowa. Nancy arrested. I get blunzed. Manhattan.
Wednesday	10/2	Today.
Thursday	10/3	Tomorrow.

I stared at the list for a while, and then erased it. I'd get those yellow gluons from Bitter today. Since I was Harry's sister and Nancy was Fletcher's wife, the police would let us into Harry's shop to look around. We'd say we wanted to inventory the valuables. And then I'd get blunzed. But if yellow gluons were as scarce as Harry said, I wouldn't have much time to maneuver. I'd need to pack everything into one fast wish. I groped for the best way to put it.

Make everything be just like it was on the morning of Friday, September 20.

No, that wouldn't work. That would just throw us all into a horrible time loop. If everything was *just like* that Friday, then it would *be* that Friday again, and the whole crazy string of events would happen over again, ending with me wishing us back to that Friday again—no, thanks. Try again.

Undo all the wishes that Harry and I have made up till now.

That would be stupid! Just for openers, I'd lose my money. Not to mention the fact that Antie—and maybe Harry too—would be dead. And I wouldn't get to do my part to start the universe. No, no. I had to get more specific.

Make my body be like it used to, and have the governor pardon Harry, Sondra and me.

That seemed fine. I made a hard copy and folded it into my purse. I fell into a light doze and dreamed about Harry and the bumblebee. I was the bee.

"Ma'am?"

I sat up and looked around. We were off the turnpike and nearing Princeton. The robot driver was talking to me.

"Do you need instructions?"

"Nnno. The otherrr llady gavve me the address."

"Of Alwin Bitter?"

"Yesss."

"Well, what do you want, then? I was sleeping."

"I'm bored. Do you knnow anny logic puzzles?"

I glanced at the meter. A hundred and sixty-seven dollars now. Two hundred bucks and I was supposed to entertain the driver as well?

"No, I don't know any logic puzzles." The robot

made such a disappointed sound that I relented. "Well, maybe I do. What about this one. A genie promises a man that he can have exactly one wish come true. Now, what if the man's one wish is that he gets all the wishes he wants?"

"He willl get all the wishes he wannts."

"But remember! An initial condition is that he is allowed to have only one wish."

"I ssseee. So he willl get nno wishes."

"But he was supposed to get one wish."

"Butt perhaps the mann's rreal wish was that he get nno wishes at all. He does gett his wissh."

"But then he doesn't."

"I ssee. Thannk you forr the puzzle. I willl ponderr it."

25

Levels of Uncertainty

"Would you like some iced tea . . . Mr. Fletcher?"

"Thank you, Mrs. Bitter. I would."

The four of us were sitting in their living room. Five of us, counting Serena. She was sitting on my lap, though she didn't understand who I was supposed to be. I took her little arms and clapped her hands together. She laughed gaily; at least I could still make my daughter laugh.

"So the wishes haven't worked out well?" Bitter asked me.

"Not entirely. I'm stuck in a woman's body, and we're all in trouble with the police."

"Nancy was telling me a little about the machine that you and Harry Gerber built. How did you two come to invent it?"

"Well . . . that's a little complicated." I paused,

trying to think how to say it. "The plans for the blunzer came to Harry in a dream. He dreamed he saw someone who told him how to build it. So he went ahead and built it, and later I got blunzed. I didn't understand the machine, but after I got blunzed I was able to figure out the plans by looking at the machine and reading Harry's mind. So then I went back in time and put the plans in Harry's mind while he was dreaming. I was the person he saw in his dream to begin with. It's a circle. The universe made it happen, is what Harry says. He says the universe was using us to excite itself."

"Like a writer reading his own dirty books," sniggered Nancy. She didn't take me seriously anymore.

"More like a fountain that recycles its water." I frowned. "Or a battery that runs its own re-charger."

"The self-generative Absolute," said Bitter non-committally. His wife, Sybil, came back from the kitchen with four glasses of iced tea on a tray. She was a slender lady whose tall body shaped a grace-ful S-curve. She kept giving me curious looks—as if I were some kind of carnival freak.

"I've come to ask for your help," I told Bitter. "Harry says that with your connections here you might be able to get me some yellow gluons. Each color of gluon just works once, and we've already used the red kind and the blue kind. I need the yellow gluons so I can activate the blunzer one last time and—"

"Dr. Bitter's the one to ask?" Nancy exclaimed.

"I hadn't realized. What a wonderful coincidence! Will you help us, Alwin?"

"I don't know if I should. Things aren't perfect for you now—but they could, after all, be much worse."

"I'll do the wishing," proposed Nancy. "I won't ask for anything stupid like Harry and Joe did."

"What would *you* ask for?" I demanded angrily. Serena left my lap for safer territory.

"Just leave it to me, *Susan*."

"No way! I've thought this through, Nancy, and I know just what—"

"I will try to get you the gluons," interrupted Bitter. "On the condition that Nancy be the one to make the wish. I like Nancy."

Nancy and the white-haired old man exchanged a smile. Sitting here in my tailored tweed earthtone suit I felt like a fool. I needed help and these people were playing games with me.

"I don't think you understand what kind of forces we're dealing with, Dr. Bitter." I rapped out his name like a curse.

"Call me Alwin. Let's all be friends here. What kinds of forces *are* we dealing with, Joe? How do you and Harry think the blunzer functions?"

"Why do you ask? If you're so enlightened, you already know all about it. You just want to laugh at me, don't you?"

"No, please!" Bitter made a placating gesture with both hands. "I'm simply asking for information. It is obvious that your machine works. I'm curious about the method. Tell it to me as best you can."

"A person gets blunzed by having the value of

Planck's constant change in his brain tissue," I began.

"*Her* brain," interrupted Nancy.

"The *person's* brain," I snarled. "Can you shut up and let me explain it just one time? The idea is to treat the gluons so they become an utterly feature-less fluid known as Planck juice. This fluid is in what might be termed a *second-order quantum state*. It is doubly indeterminate. Not only is there the usual indeterminacy at the scale of Planck's constant, there is a second-order indeterminacy: *an indetermi-nacy in the actual value of Planck's constant.*" Harry and the blunzer had taught me well.

"So this Planck juice is, so to speak, unsure of the value of Planck's constant?" asked Bitter.

"Correct. It is fed into a one-meter-long subether wave guide leading to the subject's brain. In the wave guide, the field symmetry breaks, and the Planck juice becomes the carrier of a new value of Planck's constant 'seeing' the wave guide's one-meter length, the fluid chooses that for the new Planck length."

"One meter," said Bitter, measuring the length out with his hands. Instead of ten-to-the-minus-thirty-third centimeters. "That's a very large amplification."

"One hundred decillion fold," I confirmed. "When the fluid is injected into the subject's brain, the entire brain becomes arbitrarily indeterminate, for the brain's size is now less than the one-meter Planck length. The personality associated with the brain becomes able to do anything whatsoever."

"A third-order uncertainty," mused Bitter. "An ingenious device. And you say that *you* invented it?"

"No one invented it, I tell you. I got it from

Harry and Harry got it from me. It made us build it."

"Yet it only wants to work three times," said Bitter, sitting back in his chair. "What do you think of all this, Sybil?"

"I think you're right to let Nancy have the third wish," said Bitter's wife. She had lighted a cigarette and was holding her head tilted back to keep the smoke out of her eyes. "It's like a fairy tale. Do you remember the story of the magic fish that we read, Serena?"

"Yus."

"How does it go?" asked Nancy.

"Like this," said old Sybil. "A poor fisherman catches a magic fish. The fish says, 'Put me back in the water and you can have anything you want.' So the fisherman throws the magic fish back in the water. When he gets home to his little hut, he tells his wife. The wife says she wants to live in a mansion. So the fisherman goes back to the ocean and asks the fish for a mansion. Fine. When the fisherman gets home, there's a mansion, but his wife isn't satisfied for long. 'This isn't enough,' she says. 'I want to be a queen in a castle.' So the fisherman goes back to the ocean and calls to the fish again. When he gets home, his wife is a queen in a castle, but she still isn't happy. 'I want to be empress of the sun and the moon,' she says. Well, the fisherman goes back to yell for the magic fish again, but this time the fish gets mad and takes everything away."

"It was the wife's fault!" I exclaimed. "It was the wife's fault that they ended up with nothing."

"It wasn't the wife who kept going back to bother the magic fish," said Sybil, looking at me through a haze of smoke. "The fisherman should have thought for himself. I know another three-wish fairy tale, too."

"I've heard it," I interrupted. " 'The Peasant and the Sausage.' "

"Yes," said Sybil. "And I suppose you blame the wife in that one too, don't you, Joe?" She was just backing up Nancy because they were both women.

"Of course it was the wife's fault. If she hadn't asked for that stupid sausage—"

"And what if the husband hadn't been so mean? They would have had two good wishes left. A husband should think for himself and keep his temper."

I was going to yell something back, but Bitter interrupted me. "Don't try to argue with Sybil. It's hopeless. I'll try and get you the yellow gluons, Joe, but Nancy will have to be the one to get blunzed."

"All right," I sighed. "But what are you going to wish for, Nancy? Make sure you get me back my right body, and get Harry and Sondra and me out of trouble with the law."

"I'll wish what I like," said Nancy tartly. That Sybil was a bad example, a real troublemaker.

"I made a big wish once," said Alwin suddenly. "It was a long time ago. I was involved with a dangerous experiment—an experiment even more dangerous than yours, Joe. It gave me endless power, but the world was being destroyed. I had to use my power to renormalize reality. I had to use my power to get rid of my power."

"Do all the wish stories have to end that way?" protested Nancy. "With everyone back where they started?"

"One could argue that the world is perfect just as it is," said Bitter. "The world is the sum of all our wishes about it. And all of us are aspects of the One."

"I understand," said Nancy softly. "I understand, Alwin."

"Well, I sure don't," I said, rising to my feet. My skirt was rucked up awkwardly around my waist. I patted at my big hips, trying to smooth the fabric down. "Come on, Dr. Bitter, less talk and more action. Let's go get those gluons."

"All right. I'll make a phone call first."

Nancy and I said goodbye to Serena while Bitter made his call. Sybil kept staring at me in curiosity. She seemed fascinated by the idea of a man trying to move a woman's body around.

"Don't you like being a woman?" she asked me finally.

"No, it's too hard. There's a fairy tale about that too, isn't there?"

"That's right," said Sybil. " 'The Farmer Who Would Keep House.' " Her soft eyes were dancing and her broad mouth was amused. It was hard to stay mad at this woman.

"Can you watch Serena just a little longer?" asked Nancy.

"I have to go meet a friend," said Sybil. "But my daughter Ida will be home from school soon. She'll keep an eye on Serena. Make a good wish, Nancy!"

"It's all set," said Bitter, coming back into the room. "Tri Lu has some yellow gluons you can have for one million dollars."

"Let's go."

Alwin and Nancy and I set out on foot. Lu's office wasn't far.

25
I Do It

TRI Lu had big teeth, a skinny yellow face, and an unruly shock of dry, black hair. It was love at first sight.

"Ah Joe Fletcher you?" Long, jerky laughter. "You very lucky!" More laughter. He stuck out his thumb and pinkie and put his hand to his ear—miming a telephone call. "I talk Dr. Baumgard. He very angry you."

"Has he called the police?"

"He want information you promise. He want right away. You sit my lap now, Joe. I call." He was laughing again, pulling in lungfuls of air between each spasm. *Hohawhaha-gasp-hohawhahaha-gasp.* Finally it turned into a coughing fit and he buried his face in his hands. He was embarrassed by how much he wanted me.

"Are you sure this is the right guy?" I asked old Bitter.

"Yes. He's our finest experimentalist. If he can't help you, no one can."

"I don't like the way he looks at you, Joe," said Nancy.

Nervously I reached up to ruffle my hair. Tri Lu had recovered now. He was watching me. He was ready to eat me alive, drumsticks first.

"Why don't you two wait outside," I told Nancy and Alwin. "Dr. Lu and I will work this out."

"Are you sure?"

"Yes. Please leave us alone till I call you. Go for a walk or something."

They went out and I closed the office door. I leaned against it, hands behind my back, and gave Tri Lu my biggest smile. He smiled back.

"Come here, Joe. I dial."

I went and sat in Lu's lap while he dialed Baumgard's number. It seemed like the easiest thing to do. Hell, I had nothing to be scared of. I had twenty pounds on the guy, easy.

"I hope I'm not too heavy for you, Dr. Lu."

He handed me the receiver and threw his arms around me. "Good fat American cowgirl. I love."

"Hello?" quacked the little voice on the phone. "Baumgard here."

"Dana. This is Joe Fletcher." Lu had his hands on my breasts. The nipples were starting to tingle. It was hard to concentrate on the secret of the universe. "I'm in Tri Lu's office, and he said I should call you, so . . ." I broke off in a squeal as Lu's hungry Vietnamese fingers dug too far into my ripe American flesh.

"You sound odd, Fletcher. Has something happened to you?"

"I'll say. Never mind. I wanted to call you about the reason why things exist."

"The experiment was a success?"

"Yes. The universe is a sort of perpetual motion machine. It funnels energy from the future back to the past. The universe is a self-excited system."

A pause. Then, "That's not enough, Fletcher. Where does the whole system come from at all? The world-snake bites its tail—fine. Where did the snake come from?"

Lu was trying to force his hand between my thighs now. I had my knees pressed tight together, but I could feel myself weakening. This skinny little guy was awfully cute. "What did you say, Dana?"

"Where does the self-generating universe come from?"

"Uh—I don't know. I didn't ask. I just looked at the Big Bang. I helped the universe make the Big Bang."

"This won't do, Fletcher. I'm in trouble over the missing gluons. I should call the police and—"

"Would you take a million dollars?" Lu was straining his face upward toward mine for a kiss. I let him have one. He tasted nice. I noticed I still had the phone in my hand. Oh, yes, Baumgard. "I'll give you a million dollars," I repeated and hung up.

I made sure the office door was locked, and then I let Tri Lu take off all my clothes. He swarmed onto me like an excited tick. I was huge and beautiful. We made love. I was glad to finally do it. I was glad to be a sexy woman.

An hour passed, maybe more. The office windows had venetian blinds, and the afternoon sun was striping us with shadows. I sat up, remembering Nancy. Time to get dressed again, time to cover up.

I watched Tri Lu stepping awkwardly into his underwear. I loved him. He was a person, a person who wanted to be happy. I was happy, but I still wanted something more. I wanted yellow gluons.

"I have two million dollars," I said, taking the packets of bills from my purse. "One for you, one for Dana."

"Silly paper. Not worth like good love me you." He gave me one of his all-purpose smiles. His long hair stuck straight up from the top of his head.

"Oh, Lu." I hugged him one last time. "Thank you so much."

"I thank more. Soft cowgirl." He kissed his fingers and touched my breasts. I patted his cheek and then took out my compact to check my makeup. Hopelessly smeared. Nancy would know. Well, let her. I had to use my femaleness at least once, didn't I?

We left the money on Lu's desk and took the elevator down to the basement laboratory. There was a giant linear accelerator there, a silver tube stretching off down a tunnel leading out of the basement. Our end of the accelerator—the business end—was surrounded by a thicket of machinery. To one side of the machinery was a table littered with papers and rubber bands.

"Quark and gluon," Lu said, stepping over to the table. "Look, Joe." He handed me a little model, a single band of rubber with rubber-cement globs at either end. The blackened globs were the size of acorns.

"Like quark," said Lu, pointing to one of the globs. "Gluon connect." He strummed the rubber band.

I toyed with the little model for a minute. As long as the quark-globs were near each other, they experienced no particular attraction. But if you tried to pull them apart, the connecting band stretched tighter and tighter, drawing the quarks back together.

"If cut here," said Lu, pointing at the middle of the band, "make two new quark."

If the gluon was a band holding the quarks together, the quarks could be thought of as the ends of the gluon-band. Cutting the band would make two new loose ends, two new quarks.

"Instead I pinch off," said Lu, handing me a different model. It was like the first one, except here the connecting gluon-band had been folded back to meet itself and form a loop. If you pinched the loop free, you'd get a circular gluon-band, a free gluon with no quarks attached.

"Two year work," said Lu, starting to laugh again. He was handing me a little magnetic bottle from a cabinet by the accelerator. "One thirtieth gram yellow gluons. Million dollar." His laughter slid into another coughing fit.

I opened the little bottle and looked inside. The gluons were yellow as the sun in water, yellow as Lu, yellow as an ear of corn. Hot, golden yellow. I put the bottle in my purse.

We said our goodbyes and I left the physics building to look for Nancy. I found her with Alwin on a stone bench a few hundred meters off. Leaves were blowing around, and the bright air was like cold water.

"You're a mess," said Nancy. "What took so long?"

I didn't answer. Instead I held up the gluons. "Here they are. Enough gluons for two and a half seconds. Have you figured out your wish?"

"I want to know what you did to smear your makeup like that, Joe."

"You know. I had to. I had to do it, Nancy."

"God, you're disgusting." She turned her face down and picked at a spot on her pants. Suddenly we were both in tears.

"I'm sorry, Nancy. I'm sorry I'm so twisted up. But the gluons will make everything right again. I'm sure they will." I sat down on Bitter's other side. "Tell her, Alwin. Tell her I love her."

"You tell her," said Bitter, getting to his feet. "I'm going home."

So I told Nancy that I loved her. I told her I wanted things to be the same again, only better. I told her I'd only let Lu have me so he would sell me the gluons. After a while Nancy believed me. A little longer, and I believed it too.

"So what are you going to wish for?" I asked when we'd finished making up.

"I was talking to Alwin and—I think I have an

idea," said Nancy. "But I want to make sure I do it right. Could you explain about the Planck length again?"

"The Planck length is ordinarily about 10^{-33} centimeters," I said. "Much smaller than an atom or an elementary particle. The Planck length is the size scale below which ordinary physics breaks down. There's no cause and effect for things smaller than Planck length. There's total uncertainty down there, and anything can happen. Now, the idea behind the blunzer is to magnify the Planck length all the way up to one meter. When you get blunzed, the Planck length will get that big in a region around your head. So for a few seconds you'll be in a zone of total uncertainty. Anything you want to have happen will be true."

"What if the Planck length blew up to ten meters? Couldn't several people get blunzed at once then?"

"Yeah, I gucss so. Only one person really needs to get the injection. The brain acts as a kind of amplifier."

"What injection?"

"The final stage of getting blunzed is where a needle jabs in through your fontanelle—you know, where Serena had her soft spot?"

"Right on top of my head?" Instinctively Nancy raised her hand to her scalp. "Does it hurt?"

"No, not really. You hear a sort of crunching, but it doesn't hurt. And then you're blunzed."

"You say I'll only have two seconds?"

"Two and two-fifths, actually. Now will you tell me what your wish is going to be?"

"No. Alwin told me not to. He said you might try to change my mind."

"Well, I'm not going to argue with you," I sighed. "Just make sure I get my body back. Shall we fly to New Brunswick?"

"Okay."

Nancy lay down on the ground, I sat on her butt, and we took off.

27

Nancy's Wish

WITHOUT a windfoil, Nancy couldn't fly as fast as Sondra had. We got up to a few hundred meters and followed the turnpike north to New Brunswick. When we were about halfway there, I spotted a big black dot approaching. A hawk? A guided missile?

No, it was Sondra, fresh out of the Carteret Correctional Center. She cruised up to us and we hovered there together for a minute.

"Isn't flying fun, Nancy?" said Sondra. Her face was flushed with excitement. "They let me out into the exercise yard and I took off. I'm going to see Alwin."

"We just saw him," I said. "He helped me get some more gluons."

"And I asked him what to wish for," added Nancy. "I get to make the wish."

"Why don't you just wish for lots of wishes?" Sondra suggested. "Wish for all the wishes we want."

"That's too vague," I protested. "I don't think wishes about wishing are allowed."

"It's just a machine," said Sondra. "Not a leprechaun or something. Nancy ought to ask for a hundred wishes."

The two women were hovering side by side. With the bright sun, I felt like a bather on a float. There were fields below us and, off to the right, the Jersey Turnpike, with cars crawling like ants.

"Don't worry, Sondra," said Nancy. "I'm going to ask for something really big. I think my wish is the real reason the blunzer made itself."

"What's your wish?" I asked again. But Nancy still refused to tell me.

"How's Harry?" Sondra asked me.

"I saw him this morning. He's in the Rahway prison. He wants to get out."

"I just wish those seventeen people hadn't died," said Sondra. "I feel bad about them. If I could wish one thing, I'd wish for them to be alive again. Nancy, do you think—"

"She's only going to have about two seconds," I interrupted. "And the main thing is to get my body back. She'll try to fix up our legal troubles too, but—"

"Leave it to me," said Nancy. "I know just what to do."

Some schoolchildren in the fields below had noticed us. Their tiny shouts floated up on the gentle autumn breezes.

"You know," said Sondra, "I keep having trouble believing I can fly. I really have to concentrate to keep from falling down. Like in a flying dream. Don't you feel that too, Nancy?"

"Hey," I interrupted anxiously. "That's no way to be thinking right now."

" . . . and just drop like a stone," Nancy mused. "If suddenly you forget how. Yeah, I can really feel that, Sondra. How about you, Joe?"

"Hey, look, girls, this is—" A farmer drove his pickup into the field beneath us and got out with a rifle. There came a faint popping of gunfire.

We said a hurried goodbye to Sondra and flew the rest of the way to New Brunswick. Nancy came in low and touched down in a parking lot near Harry's place. At first I thought no one had noticed us, but then an old bum came stumbling over.

"Take me for a ride, angels." He had the weather-beaten skin of a sailor. "Take me out to sea." He seemed deranged, albeit strong enough to cause serious trouble.

"Go away," I said curtly. "Leave us alone." We started out of the parking lot with the bum tagging along after us.

"Give me something," he begged. "I need money to buy a pet fish."

"Here." I drew a ten-dollar bill out of my handbag and gave it to him. "Now beat it."

"Thank you, fish angel."

The windows of Harry's store were boarded up. There was a shiny black car parked in front. When Nancy and I tried the shop's door, it flew open, revealing a fit-looking man in a black suit. He held a pistol in one hand. "Who are you?" he demanded.

"Susan Gerber and Nancy Fletcher," I said. "We

want to make sure you don't steal anything from our men."

"I'm Joseph Fletcher's wife," amplified Nancy. "And this is Harry Gerber's sister. We'd like to get a few personal effects and make an inventory."

The man gave a sharp whistle and pulled us in. The door slammed shut behind us. Inside was another man in black. He'd been guarding the back door. Both of them were armed. They said they were from the government.

"Why won't your brother talk?" the first man asked me. "His device has an enormous potential to enhance our national security."

"Harry never tells me what he's doing," I simpered. "Not that *I* could understand it anyway."

"And what about you?" the second man asked Nancy. "Where is your husband hiding?"

"I bet it's somewhere hot and wet," said Nancy. "My husband loves that kind of place. Some overgrown delta at the mouth of a river. Who knows? You're the cops, not me."

"I could use a tropical vacation myself," said the second man in black. "I'd like to be in the Bahamas." He turned to his partner. "How about you, Jack?"

"If I had my druthers," said the first man in black, "I'd be camping out in the Rockies right now."

They'd fallen for our story and had loosened up a little. I kept giving them nice smiles.

"Can we look around now?" I asked. "We'd like to start upstairs and then check over the workshop."

"We'll have to search your purses for weapons."

"Fine." I opened my purse. There was my compact in there, the Susan Gerber IDs, some more money, and the magnetic bottle of gluons.

"What's this?" asked the first man in black, picking up the bottle.

"That's—that's my deodorant."

"Oh. Sorry."

They let us go upstairs alone; it was the workshop they were really interested in guarding.

"How are we going to get rid of them?" Nancy whispered.

"Maybe we should get knives from the kitchen?"

"No killing, Joe. You'll just get us in even more trouble. And those men have guns."

"So what do we do? Seduce them?"

"Why don't we start a fire up here? They'll run up to put it out and then we can lock ourselves in the workshop. Does it take long to start the blunzer?"

"Not that long. If we can get ourselves locked in the workshop, we'll have time before they break in." We wandered into the bedroom.

"Let's light Harry's bed," suggested Nancy. "It's nice and greasy."

"You don't like Harry, do you, Nancy?"

"Why should I? He doesn't like me." She found a half-empty bottle of over proof vodka and poured it out on Harry's pillow. "This ought to help. Can you find a match?"

I found some matches in the kitchen, and another bottle of vodka. I brought a bunch of newspapers as well. Nancy had a whole plan of action figured out now. It sounded good to me.

We got the bed sluggishly burning. It gave off a lot of smoke. Nancy flew up to the ceiling by the bedroom door. She was holding a thick broom handle.

When the smoke started to trickle down the stairs to the shop, I ripped open my blouse and began screaming. "There's another Gary-brain up here! Oh, help me!" I stood at the head of the stairs looking desperate.

"I'll save you!" shouted one of the men in black. He came surging up the stairs, and I pretended to stagger backwards into the smoke-filled bedroom. Nancy was waiting right overhead, broomstick at the ready. When the man in black came in, I embraced him and held him steady so Nancy could whack him on the top of the head. It took three whacks to knock him out.

I got the gun out of his hand, shoved it under my skirt's waistband, and ran downstairs. I ran right into the other man in black. "One of those brains is loose up there," I cried. "I think it got Mrs. Fletcher!"

The man pushed past me. I hurried into the shop and locked the door to the stairs. Then I went to open the front door. Nancy was waiting out there. She'd flown down from Harry's bedroom window.

We ran into the workshop and got that door locked, too. Antie was in the workshop, turned off and lying on her side. I switched her power on and we got to work on the blunzing machinery. You could hear the footsteps of the men in black running around upstairs. They were busy putting out the fire.

"Go lie on that table in the blunzing chamber," I

told Nancy. "Put on the breathing mask and get ready for the shot."

"I'm scared, Joe."

"Do you want me to go instead of you?"

"No. I'll do it." For the first time today Nancy kissed me. "I'll make a better world, Joe."

"The microwave cavity is ready," called Antie.

"Get the gluons from my purse!" I shouted. "Good luck, Nancy."

Now Nancy was in the blunzing chamber. I switched on the sheathing field. Antie poured the gluons into the microwave. There was noise out in the shop. I fired a random gunshot through the door. Antie fed the gluons into the vortex coil.

Noise and confusion took over. For the third and final time, someone got blunzed—but not just Nancy.

Everyone got blunzed this time, everyone on Earth. For that was Nancy's wish: that the Planck length be ten thousand kilometers big for the 2.4 seconds that her gluons lasted. Everyone got to make a wish at once.

28
Earthly Delights

THE guards were gone and it was raining outside—raining fish. The big rain-fish would hit the pavement, flop a little, and then melt into water.

"You really did it," I said to Nancy. I had my arm around her, and she was leaning against my long, lean frame. I was back to normal.

"Where's Harry?" asked the old woman behind us. Antie had turned herself into a flesh-and-blood copy of Harry's dead mother. The blunzing had even affected her. Nancy's little echowomen had flown out of the chamber and helped each of us make our wish. Antie's had been *to be just like Harry's mother.* I wondered what kinds of wishes everyone else had made. The rain-fish were probably the idea of the crazy old sailor we'd seen. Everyone had gotten what they wanted most. "Where's Harry?" repeated Antie.

I waited for Nancy to answer, but she seemed too drained. Her feat had taken a lot out of her.

"I don't know where Harry is," I told Antie. "He probably got himself out of prison. Maybe he'll turn up here soon."

"You ought to hide," fretted the old woman. "Now that the police can recognize you again."

"That's all fixed," I reassured her. "After I changed my body I got us all pardons from the governor. And I bet Sondra brought those seventeen dead people back to life."

"That's right," murmured Nancy. "And the men in black took their vacations. One to the Bahamas and one to the Rockies."

A man-sized beetle marched past, the rain of fish beating on his iridescent green back. What a weirdo *he* must have been. Leaning out the door, I could see that it was sunny down by the railroad station. A fish struck me on the head and splatted onto the sidewalk.

"Let's find an umbrella and take a walk." I suggested.

"I'm waiting here for Harry," said Antie stubbornly. "And I have to clean up the mess in his bedroom."

"Fine. Nancy and I'll go out alone."

We got an umbrella and went outside. There was a startling roar as a race car shot past, its tires throwing up sheets of fish-water. It looked like an Indy 500 racer—which is what it probably was. A block away from the store I spotted the old sailor, staring up into the sky and catching fish in his mouth. Another block and we were in sunlight. I folded up the umbrella and looked around.

The train station had been transformed into a graceful lacework of metal and glass, a veritable crystal palace of transportation. A fine steam locomotive was just pulling in.

"Isn't she a beauty?" yelled the engineer, leaning out and waving. "I've always wanted to run one of these!" We smiled and waved back.

The Terminal Bar across the street had become a huge old saloon of the same period as the locomotive. You could hear a honky-tonk piano inside. The mustached bartender stood in the door, grinning and holding an inexhaustible schooner of beer. He gave us a happy salute. It was almost like being in Disneyland—except everything was real.

"Did everyone make good wishes?" I asked Nancy.

"Yes," she smiled. "I made sure they did."

"But how?"

"I sent out my echowomen. I sent one to watch each person on Earth. If I could see a mean wish in someone's mind, I reached in and made them change it. And if two people's wishes conflicted, I made one of them change too."

Farther down the street was a sidewalk café—formerly a scuzzy German coffee shop. I recognized the owner sitting at one of the tables and eating a roast chicken.

"There's a buffet inside," he called to us. "Help yourself. I'll make out the bill later."

"Are you hungry?" I asked Nancy.

She nodded and sat down at one of the sunny tables. I went into the café and filled two plates. I brought them out and then fetched some white wine and soda.

We ate in silence for a minute. It was the best

food I'd ever tasted. One of the things on my plate was a crisp white veal sausage. I held it up for Nancy to see, remembering the fable.

She laughed and patted my hand. "You see, Joe? It's not so bad to ask for simple things."

"Do you know what each person wished?"

"No, not anymore. While I was blunzed I knew, sort of. I sent my echowomen everywhere, like Alwin said I should. I made the Planck length big enough to cover the whole Earth, and I helped everyone make his or her wish."

"Do people know it was you? You'll be treated like a queen!"

"No, no. You know how small most of the echoes are. People couldn't see me. And I wouldn't *want* them to know it was me, because then they'd ask me to do it again."

"Yeah. And we can't do it again. There's only three colors of gluon, and each color only works once." An attractive young couple floated down out of the sky to sit at a table nearby. Glancing up, I could see a number of people flying around overhead. The power of flight seemed to be a fairly common wish.

"I wonder what Harry wished for," I mused. "Do you know?"

"I meant to check, but he was already gone by the time I got to him. He was like you—he knew right away he'd been blunzed, and he acted on it."

"He wasn't in Rahway anymore?"

"He left our space, so far as I could tell. Look at those two!"

Another couple had joined the crowd at the café—a beautiful red-haired woman and a man who was only three inches high. The man was perched in the redhead's décolletage like a prince on a balcony. It looked like a good place to be.

More and more people were out in the street now, everyone chattering and looking around to see what the others had done. There were many more beautiful men and women than was normal for New Brunswick; beauty was obviously a wish even more popular than flight. Lots of people wore jewels as well, and I noticed several men drawing out big wads of cash.

"All my money's going to be worthless," I suddenly realized. "Everybody and his brother must have asked for a million dollars."

"Yes," said Nancy. "But we've still got our penthouse."

"But what are we going to live on? I can't go back to working at Softech."

"Go back in business with Harry," suggested Nancy. "If you can find him."

"Yeah, that's a thought." I was distracted again by a passerby, this one a man running at what must have been thirty miles per hour. "Look at that guy go!"

"A lot of beauties, a lot of millionaires, a lot of great athletes," said Nancy. "Can I have some more wine, please?"

A giant breast rolled past, followed by a man with four arms. Shiny cars—antique and futuristic alike—buzzed this way and that. In a doorway across the street lay a man slumped in some interminable ecstasy. In the distance I heard music playing.

"How about Alwin Bitter? What did he wish for?"

Nancy's eyes danced above her tilted wineglass. "Alwin—Alwin is an altruist," she said, setting down her glass. "He wished for this all to happen."

"But the blunzer made itself. It was a cause-and-effect loop with Harry and me in it."

"Even so, you and Harry and the loop had to come from somewhere. Alwin wished you into existence."

"I don't believe that, Nancy, do you?"

"I don't know. What's important is that now everyone will be happy for quite a while, and maybe later—even if the changes all wear off—people will still remember how to be happy. I thought it was worth a try."

A machine that seemed to be a flying saucer zipped down the street and hovered by our cafe. A hatch opened and family of little green "Martians" hopped out. They talked with New Jersey accents.

"This sure is fun, Nancy. Did you happen to notice what Serena wished for?"

"A pet rabbit and a box of candy."

"Sweet. Maybe we better fly down to Princeton and pick her up. You can still fly, can't you?"

"Sure. You'll feel better to me with all that girl fat gone." Nancy reached under the table and squeezed my thigh. I drank a little more wine and smiled at her. Everyone in sight looked happy. It was like some magic Christmas party.

I waved the café owner over for the check. "How much?"

"I dunno. You got a lot of money, don't you?"

"Sure. Here, take a hundred." I fished the bill out of the purse I'd been using and handed it over.

The café owner looked at the bill with a frown. "Is this real?"

"Was the food?" I countered.

"Okay, a hundred," grumbled the owner. "But I don't like it. Why didn't *I* think of asking for money instead of a new restaurant?"

"You're better off with the restaurant," I assured him. "There's going to be inflation like you won't believe." The whole financial system was going to have to be reworked. It was going to be a mess. People wouldn't stay happy for long. The café owner stomped off to the lovers from the sky and charged them a cool grand for two cups of coffee. "Maybe you should have. tried to change human nature," I told Nancy as we stood up. "Make people nicer and more generous."

"Some people did wish that for themselves," Nancy responded. "There'll be a lot of saints around."

A man in the shape of a motorcycle went zooming past with a fur-covered woman on his saddle. Glancing after them, I noticed a building made entirely of meat: a skin-covered orifice building with people plunging in and out of its portals. I was beginning to wish for a less frantic scene.

"Well, come on, Nancy, lie down and—"

Two hands suddenly appeared in front of me. Familiar-looking hands. They grabbed me by the shoulders and yanked me into the unknown.

29

Rudy Rucker Is Watching You

You could say that everything went black, or you could say that everything went white. I was . . . elsewhere.

But not alone.

"Hey, Fletcher," came the familiar voice, "you have to help me."

"Harry? Where are we?"

"Superspace, naturally."

"What's superspace?" I felt around for my body and couldn't find it.

"Thoughtland, Fletch, the cosmos. Pure mentation. Abstract possibility. Infinite dimensions. The class of all sets. God's mind. The pre-geometric substratum. Hilbert space. Penultimate reality. White . . ."

"Cut the crap, Harry. I was having a good time till you butted in. Put me back."

"You don't want to rush back there. This is much cooler. This is eternity, Joe, this is the secret of life."

"Oh come on, Harry. I'm not interested in the secret of life. I just want to go home and be with Nancy. She and Sondra are going to be at Alwin Bitter's."

"Hold it." Contrasts appeared in the black-or-white void around me. Streamers, clumps, hazy patches. "Can you see it now?"

"I can't see anything. I might as well be looking at clouds."

"You see clouds? Wait." The fog folded in on itself. Colors appeared. Definite forms began to congeal. One of them was Harry, and one of them was me.

"That's better," I said, tentatively moving my arm. The arm disappeared.

"Your arm's in another dimension now," Harry explained. "We're in a three-dimensional cross section of infinite-dimensional superspace. If you try, you can get your arm back."

I tried. And then my arm was back, though the hand was still missing. I examined the stub where my arm ended. It looked as if my hand had been chopped right off. I could see the bone and its marrow, the muscle tissues, and the round mouths of the veins. Yet no blood was spurting out.

"Flip your wrist," urged Harry.

I flipped my wrist some funny way, and suddenly my hand was back. This was pretty interesting. I gave Harry's head a push, and watched it disappear. Peering down into his neck, I could see the insides of his lungs and stomach. But then his head snapped back.

"Where's our universe?" I asked Harry. Our two bodies seemed quite definite now, though nothing else did. Everything else was just shifting patterns of colored light.

"It's that spot there," said Harry, pointing at a small, egg-shaped blob of hazy white.

"What are all the other spots?"

"Other universes, of course. I've been here before. Briefly. When I got blunzed the first time, I came here to find the Looking-Glass World." Harry indicated a reddish patch of light near the white one that was home.

"Why are they so small?"

"That's from our position on the size axis. There's an axis for everything here."

I floated closer to our universe and peered at it. The hazy white light was patterned into whorls and dots. Galaxy clusters.

"Right now we're in a space parallel to our universe's time," said Harry, taking my arm. "But we can turn sideways."

He yanked at me and everything changed again. Now our universe egg was striped like a watermelon, filamented like a gooseberry. Bright lines stretched from one pole to the other.

"The Big Bang is down there," said Harry, pointing at one end. "See how some of the loops lead back? That's what you were doing when you got blunzed. Leading them back."

Looking more closely, I could see that our universe was really made up of a single tangled thread, a bright line that wove forward and back and in and out. It was like an endlessly knotted wire, a tangle of yarn, the Gordian knot. I looked at some of the other universes, knotty eggs all around us. We were really behind the scenes.

" . . . different axis for each property," Harry was saying.

"Can we change the scale? I'd like to be able to see Earth."

"Sure." Harry tugged my arm again, and things changed like images in a kaleidoscope. I felt dizzy and longed for something to stand on.

No sooner thought than done. We were standing in a hallway with peeling yellow walls. The universe egg floated in front of us, an infinitely detailed image in a crystal ball.

"Is this real?" I scuffed at the dirty floor. Spit, cigarette butts, hair.

"This is the transport axis. We see it our own way. I think we can get a scale change up ahead."

Walking down the hall, we passed several closed doors. I wondered who or what lay behind them. I wondered, but I didn't want to know. I kept having the feeling that we were being watched by some cool, detached intelligence just out of sight.

At the end of the hall were some rotten-looking stairs. When I put my foot on the first step, the wood broke through and scraped my leg. "We better hug the wall," I suggested. "That'll be more solid." I had the feeling that something was following us. Surely Harry and I were not the only beings to have entered Superspace.

We hurried up the decaying staircase as best we could. The universe egg stayed always a few meters ahead of us. With each step, the detail in it grew finer. I could see individual stars now, and one star that I imagined to be the Sun.

The staircase stopped abruptly. Peering over the edge, I could see down into the light-patterned chaos of before. There was a frayed rope dangling over the abyss. I reached out and pulled on it. Slowly the board we were on began to rise. It was as if we were on a painter's scaffold.

Harry helped me pull at the rope, and we rose up and up into the cluttered dark, the universe egg always just above us. You could see Earth now, North America, New Jersey—my hand slammed into a rusty pulley.

"I don't think it goes any higher, Harry." Our platform was swaying and my footing began to slip. I was sure I could hear someone breathing nearby. "Get us out of here, Harry, something's after us!"

"Wait, I'll imagine a way out. Yes!" He yanked me sideways and I heard a great creaking. A kind of bench came floating over to us. Crumbling metal struts led from the bench to some distant machinery. It was like a giant carnival ride, a cross between a roller coaster and a Ferris wheel. We both jumped for the bench, and the scaffold's rope snapped.

For a moment I thought we weren't going to make it. Hanging there for that split second I finally found the courage to look over my shoulder.

There was a man behind us, a run-down man with short hair and lambent eyes. He had the taut features and heavy stubble of a drifter. His lips were slightly parted to show his crooked teeth. Seeing me notice him, he gave the barest flicker of response—a twinge of gloating, a pulse of lust. His cool, hungry stare filled me with horror. I reached out for the now-receding bench with all my strength—and made it.

The bench was cast-iron with a leather seat. I grabbed it so hard that my tendons crackled. Harry was next to me, blandly enjoying the ride. The bench bore us higher into the gloom and the universe egg hovered before us, ever-changing. I was scared to look back again.

Princeton was in the egg, and then Alwin Bitter's house. Our bench lurched this way and that, and the house's age jerked back and forth through time. Then we were sailing along smoothly, and I could see Alwin Bitter sitting on his porch.

"Move your head," said Harry, lolling back in his seat. "Move your head and you can see him all different ways."

Following Harry's example, I turned my head this way and that. Alwin's body warped and shifted, split into cross sections and rejoined. From one angle he was no longer a flesh-body, but rather a luminous egg like the universe itself. Inside this Alwin-egg I could sense the bright cascade of his mental processes, a fleet torrent that threatened to wash my selfhood all away.

I twitched my head again and saw Alwin one hour earlier, at the moment when we'd all been blunzed. He was thinking of me and Harry, and making a wish—a strange, unbelievable wish. It was like Nancy had said—Alwin Bitter was wishing us into existence! He was making Harry and me be born and live our lives the way we had! Staggered and upset, I snapped back into an awareness of our bench.

We were on rails now, clacking through the dark like a fun-house car. Still the egg with Alwin's porch floated before us. I glanced around, anxious lest something horrible leap out at us from the dark. Fun houses have always terrified me. In my mind's eye, I kept seeing the terrible hungry face of the man who watched. Perhaps Alwin had dreamed me, but that man had dreamed Alwin.

"Let's go home, Harry. What are we here for anyway?"

"When Nancy got me blunzed, I thought the best escape would be to come here to Superspace. This is the Cosmos, not just some little universe. I like it here. It's like looking inside a radio or going down under a city's streets. You get to see how everything works."

"But a lot of it's imagination," I insisted. "The stairs and the scaffold and this bench. We're just making it up."

"That's right," said Harry with sudden venom. "*We're* making it up and not Alwin Bitter."

"You saw his wish?"

"He thinks he dreamed us up. That just—"

"Don't worry so much, Harry. There's level after level." Alwin's porch was beginning to fade. I jumped to my feet, and the bench swayed dangerously. "Come on, Harry, we're going back!"

He tried to twist away from me, but I had a good, solid grip on his hand. I leaped at the universe egg before it could change again.

30

Can It Ever Be Over?

A ND crashed down on Alwin Bitter's porch. I was holding Harry's hand, but the rest of him wasn't there.

"Help me, Alwin," I cried. "Help me drag Harry back."

Bitter grabbed me around the waist. We strained with all our might. Slowly the rest of Harry appeared: first his arm, then his shoulder, then his angry face. Finally his whole outraged body stood there: lumpy, ropy, wise old Harry. When I let go of his hand he leaped backwards, but only succeeded in falling off the porch.

"Nancy!" called Alwin. "Look who's here!"

Nancy and Serena came running out of the house. Serena was toting her new pet rabbit.

"Oh, Alwin," said Nancy, "I've been so worried. Is it all over now? Can it ever be over?"

I hugged her tight and Serena wormed in between our legs. "It's all right now, baby. Everything will be all right."

Harry was stuck in Alwin's shrubbery. It took the three of us to help him out.

"You're not the real Master of Space and Time," fumed Harry when he saw old Alwin's face. "You're not the one who made us and the blunzer and everything."

"I never said I did," said Alwin equably. "I just did my best to help things along. We all did it. No one did it. Our universe is an eigenstate."

"I bet you don't know what the Cosmos looks like," taunted Harry. The fact that he'd never even finished college made him feel defensive around real scientists. But old Bitter kept his cool.

"The Cosmos? It's like the story of the blind men and the elephant, isn't it? No one person sees the whole thing. The One is unknowable, Harry. The Cosmos does not—in any intentional sense of the word—*exist*, for—"

"Where's Sybil?" I interrupted, not wanting the argument to drag on forever. "What did she wish for?"

"She's upstairs," said Alwin happily. "She's writing a book. That was Sybil's wish, to write a good book."

"Wow," I said, impressed. "All I wished for was money and—"

"The old monetary system has been suspended," said Alwin. "Money and good looks and strength are all pretty much a drug on the market right now. As they should be. Everyone's going to have to get by on their talent."

"That's what Alwin was hoping for," Nancy explained.

All the changes were too much for me to take in. I turned to my best friend. "What are we going to do, Harry?"

Harry was already on his way into the house to look for Sondra. "What will we do?" He paused for a moment in the doorway, blinking in at the dark. "More of the same, I suppose."

KEITH LAUMER

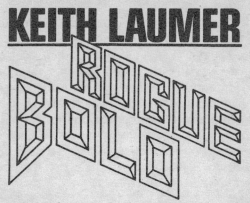

ROGUE BOLO

The Bolo Mark XX is a landgoing battleship with brains and enough firepower to destroy continents. Nothing in the universe can stand against it. Usually, it does what it's told . . .

Spivey's Find was a backwater planet, not very exciting, but a good place to live and bring up kids. Things hadn't always been that good. A few decades back, during the war with the Deng, it had seemed that the Deng might overwhelm humanity on Spivey's Find—until the Federation reinforced the colonial forces with a brand new kind of weapon: a Bolo Mark XX. After the war, the Bolo remained, shot-torn but still conscious, a memorial to the war. What thoughts brooded in its mechanical mind?

Now the Deng have returned, and humanity's only hope is that Mark XX. But the Bolo seems to have a war plan of its own, one that doesn't take humanity into account . . .

Of all Keith Laumer's works, his Bolo stories are perhaps the most eagerly awaited by hardcore SF fans, because there are so few of them. *Rogue Bolo* is the first new Bolo book in years, and it's Laumer at his best, writing about humanity's greatest weapon turning rogue!

A giant space station orbiting the Earth can be a scientific boon ... or a terrible sword of Damocles hanging over our heads. In Martin Caidin's *Killer Station*, one brief moment of sabotage transforms Station *Pleiades* into an instrument of death and destruction for millions of people. The massive space station is heading relentlessly toward Earth, and its point of impact is New York City, where it will strike with the impact of the Hiroshima Bomb. Station Commander Rush Cantrell must battle impossible odds to save his station and his crew, and put his life on the line that millions may live.

This high-tech tale of the near future is written in the tradition of Caidin's *Marooned* (which inspired the Soviet-American Apollo/Soyuz Project and became a film classic) and *Cyborg* (the basis for the hit TV series "The Six Million Dollar Man"). Barely fictional, *Killer Station* is an intensely *real* moment of the future, packed with excitement, human drama, and adventure.

Caidin's record for forecasting (and inspiring) developments in space is well-known. *Killer Station* provides another glimpse of what *may* happen with and to all of us in the next few years.

Available December 1985 from Baen Books
55996-6 • **384 pp.** • **$3.50**

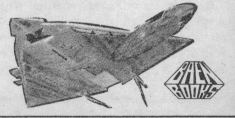